THE ELGINS' FAMILY AND FRIENDS BELIEVE IT OR NOT!

THE ELGINS' FAMILY AND FRIENDS BELIEVE IT OR NOT!

JOYCE ELGIN

THE ELGINS' FAMILY AND FRIENDS BELIEVE IT OR NOT!

iUniverse books may be ordered through booksellers or by contacting:

iUniverse
1663 Liberty Drive
Bloomington, IN 47403
www.iuniverse.com
1-800-Authors (1-800-288-4677)

ISBN: 978-1-5320-5768-7 (sc)
ISBN: 978-1-5320-5769-4 (e)

Print information available on the last page.

iUniverse rev. date: 12/12/2019

TABLE OF CONTENTS

Dear Readers,

My name is Kevin Carlson, and I am a lawyer but, most of the time I am the bodyguard for my boss, Jimmy Elgin. Tim Elgin was my best friend, and I got my information from him. Tim loved to tell tall unbelievable stories. This story is about my life with my best friend, Tim and my boss, Jimmy that ends with my son, Calvin. Do we know who we are, where we came from, or why we are here? It is a fiction story, believe it or not. You be the judge. Real names not used in this story. I tell the story, but the author wishes to remain anonymous.

I am writing this story to make you think of your family and who you are. I never thought about it, and then I met the people in this story. Now, some people may say that I have been drinking too much liquor or smoking too much weed. Well, that true, so please try to be careful with usage.

I tell you my life has not been a bore. I have lived life with all it took and enjoyed it. You become the people you see each day. So be careful of your friends. Remember you alone choose your friends and lovers. People are not replaceable so choose wisely. Don't waste time because God has given you this life and yes your parents did help too. God is the answers to all things. We need to ask God the right questions for help. He is always listening.

I have made so many mistakes, but I enjoyed every one of them. If I could do it over, I would change very little of my life because God was helping me. God is always with you, and he likes fun. Take my best friend, Tim. He was just fun to be with, but I wish I had helped him stop drinking before it was too late. I miss him every day and will never forget him.

Jimmy my boss, and friend who I will never let die. Not just because he is my friend and I protect him but because I am afraid for my children. I do not want to raise them alone. I know nothing about raising children, and I had two and maybe more. Maybe I should not have put pin holes in my boss's birth control protection and then asked to used them. Never forget to go to the drug store for supplies. But my children are the greatest gift God could have ever given me. What would life be without my children, friends, and my boss?

The unbelievable part, I think my boss is from another planet. He is a genius but has powers like reads people's minds and can disappear, reappearing in different places. I think my father was from that planet too and I have things in my head that are gold. I have no proof of this and do not want my head cut open to prove or disprove this point. So, please enjoy this fiction story, and maybe there are people on other planets that do look like you. Maybe they are not evil and don't want to kill you. Maybe they want you to stop hurting others and be your friend. Don't get too uptight about people from other worlds. As I said, it could be the liquor or smoking too much weed which I have stopped doing now.

Love,
Kevin Carlson
PS God is universal.

MAIN CHARACTERS

Aaron Erup was Margo Elgin's second husband.

Anna Elgin was Tim's sister who got shot in their kitchen.

Betty Elgin was Tim's first wife and mother of Merit and Mary; she lived in Paris.

Betsy Carlson Johnson has no mother but finds a new mother in the boy who loves her.

C-Jay Peterson is this for real or am it just dreaming. He loves her but does she love him?

Calvin Carlson is so angry but at who and why? When he finds his true love, all is good.

Cindy Elgin Peterson is the silver one, the new leader and with true love all is going her way.

Jimmy Elgin questions who he is, and he is a genius but wants his true love forever.

Kevin Carlson believes he is God's gift to women but finds he has more than looks.

King was Larry's stepfather and the man with the money.

Larry Ewing was Tim's boss and step-son of Mr. King.

Linda Ewing was the women Tim's loved and second wife. Larry's wife, Tim's boss.

Margo Elgin Erup is spoiled beyond hope and hurts the ones she loves the most to lose it all.

Michael Elgin is a genius's son and has the greatest hurt to have, but healed with love.

Micky Johnson finds true love right away and waits for the right time to act on it.

Mickey Johnson is left alone but finds friends and love just around the corner.

Sally Peterson was T-Jay's first wife, and C-Jay's mother died of cancer.

Sam Elgin has a dream to be a small-town sheriff, but life gives him so much more.

Sarah Elgin Peterson finds love is the key to happiness; good things come to those who wait.

Sylvia ??? she loves Jimmy, and he loves her, they meet in God's house, what could go wrong?

T-Jay Peterson is a rich man's son that loves white suits loses his true love to find another.

Teresa Mary Carlson is Jimmy's first daughter with his true love and Kevin second wife?

Tim Elgin starts with sadness, finds true friends but ends with sadness at his hand.

Vicki Elgin is Sam's wife who Sam thinks is a person from another planet.

Virginia Johnson was a homeless woman with her brother and sister who married Mickey.

CHAPTER ONE

TIM ELGIN WAS ASLEEP, BUT JIMMY IS COMING

The room was starting to lighten as the day began when a loud sound ripped through the quietness. What was it? Tim thought. It sounded like a gunshot, but it must be old Mr. Willie's car is backfiring again. Tim's brother, Joey fixed that car last week, and Tim tried to go back to sleep. Tim heard voices, was Dad home? Tim's Dad did not come home much since his Mom died in that car accident a few years ago. Tim heard Joey crying, but Joey never cries. Tim got out of bed and moved into the living room, still in his Superman pajamas. Anna, Tim's sister, always told Tim it was okay to be sixteen and still wear them, she was a good sister and cared for him.

"What's up?" Tim asked Joey as he'd seen the neighbors moving towards him and medical people moving around him. Anna laid on the floor still in her nightgown, blood all over her head.

Joey's eyes were filled with tears as he answered, "Anna shot." The medical staff started taking Anna away and a woman pulled Tim close to her.

Tim cried, "Anna, who will get my breakfast and when are you coming back?"

A police officer asked them, "Where can we reach your father?"

Joey replied, "I'll get the phone number later, I am feeling sick." Joey then took Tim into his bedroom saying, "Don't tell them we don't know where Dad is or they will take us to the home for children without parents. I am old enough to take care of us."

Tim questioned, "Where is Anna going and when will she be back?"

Joey answered in a low voice, "Anna is not coming back. She is in heaven with Mom." All Tim could think about was how much he missed his Mom.

As a police officer entered Tim's room, Tim asked, "Why, Joey?"

The police officer replied, "I don't know, just a drive-by shooting. Drug dealers fighting in the streets and a shot went through the window of this old house. Anna was just in the wrong place at the wrong time." Tim and Joey cried, but they cried together.

Before they knew it, their dad was home giving orders to Joey on what he needed to do. They got the least expensive casket with a plot next to their Mother's. Tim picked out three dozen pink roses. There was only three of them left now. Tim's Mother had four dozen red roses for her funeral from them.

Then came the funeral and the whole town came but Tim liked nothing about it. Joey came with his girlfriend, Sue. They had a baby boy, and that was all Joey wanted to talk about to his Dad. Cousin Jimmy came over to talk to Tim, but Tim just walked away from him to a place alone.

Then Tim felt a hand on his shoulder; it was Joey who said, "It is not your fault little brother."

They walked back into Mr. King's house. His wife had been shot too about the same time their mother died in that car accident. Mr. King had just married Larry's mother the night Anna got shot. Larry came out and asked, "Is there anything I can do for you, Tim?"

Tim replied, "I wish we had all this food at my home." Larry then called a man over and had him wrap up most of the food to take to Tim's home.

The next day Tim's Dad went to see a lawyer so Joey could take care of Tim while he was trucking. Their father drove an eighteen wheeler to the west coast. He would be gone a lot. Joey had his girlfriend, Sue move in with the baby. Sue was a good cook. Joey got a new job with Larry at this new company, Larry and his stepbrother started with Mr. King's money.

Joey had to also go to college for his new job, so Tim with Sue and the baby were home alone a lot. But Joey did get a paycheck, and Larry paid for his college. The guys Joey worked with were nice, and they came over all the time even for Tim's birthday. They would drink beer and eat cake. Tim got a card from his dad with twenty dollars in it for his birthday, but the card was mailed from town. Tim wonder why his dad did not just stop at home and give him the card? Tim was sick a lot and had been that way since the day he was born but why? Things just got worse.

On the way home from church, Joey stopped the car and said, "Tim, we need more money, so I am going to get our cousin Jimmy to live with us. He can get a job after school and weekends."

Tim cried, "No, I hate Jimmy." But Joey said no more and home they went. Thanksgiving and Christmas came still no Jimmy. Tim was sure Joey forgot all about Jimmy, but then after the holiday break, he came home to find Sue crying.

Tim asked, "What is wrong?"

Sue replied, "I am having a baby."

Tim replied, "No, you already have a baby, Jr. Joey." But Sue just cried more so when Joey got home Tim went to talk to him. Joey came in with a hand full of books and papers which he put down on the table to start work. Tim said, "Sue was crying that she is going to have another baby, but you already have a baby, Jr. Joey."

Joey looked up very sadly and said, "It does not work that way, and when you are older, I will explain it to you. Sue and I will marry soon, but first I have to get Jimmy to live with us. We have all these bills to pay; there is the heat, lights, telephone, trash, sewer, and insurance on house, car, myself. Then the hospital bills for you, car and house payments, taxes on the house, and Mom and Anna's funeral. Oh, yes food and gas, my paycheck is not enough. Jimmy can bring in extra income. We need this so Sue and I can marry before the new baby comes."

Tim asked, "What about the money Dad sends us?"

Joey answered, "Dad has not sent us any money since Anna died. And even before that, it was not very often. That is why I worked at the gas station and Anna at the café. Be nice to Jimmy. Women want us all to get along. I sent you that money for your birthday and the card."

Tim tried again, "I can work. I am older than Jimmy." Joey just shook his head no and said no more.

The next day Tim went to Sue and said, "I do not want Jimmy here. Please talk to Joey. I know he will listen to you."

Sue looked up at Tim very sad, saying, "I can't do that. Joey has too many bills to pay out of his paycheck, and me with the baby cost more. The baby is due in April, and the doctor thinks it may be twins."

Tim was overwhelmed. "Twins, two babies at one time. Talk to Larry; he gives us money. We don't need Jimmy!"

Sue replied, "Larry has been very kind, but he has two children and a young wife. He gets his money from his stepfather and must have his stepbrother as his partner. Larry's stepbrother is very spoiled and unreasonable. Larry has the good ideas and workers."

"What does Joey do for Larry? What kind of business is it?" Tim asked.

"I don't know, but Joey does some mechanical work, which he needs college to keep his job. That is Larry's stepbrother's rules not Larry's," Sue answered.

Tim tried one more time, "How do you feel about Jimmy coming to live with us? More work for you. And he is a real smart ass."

"I heard Jimmy is a handful, but we need the money. Try to be nice to him. He has had a hard life. Jimmy and you are about the same age. You could be good friends," Sue said to Tim.

Tim screamed, "No way, I will never be nice to him." Tim left for his bedroom, but about an hour later Joey knocked on his door.

Joey asked, "May I come in to talk with you?"

Tim replied, Why not, you make all the rules."

Joey came in and sat on Tim's bed saying, "Little brother, don't make this hard for me. Sue and I got to get married. Please do this for Sue. She is a great person." Then Joey kissed Tim's forehead and left the room.

That Saturday morning Joey left to get cousin, Jimmy. Tim watched out the window. Tim had liked his family now, why did it have to change? Sue worked all day on getting Jimmy's bedroom ready for him. Tim was sad all day. It was supper time when Joey came home with Jimmy. Jimmy looked taller with his blue eyes and dark hair, Tim thought, now girls will never look at him. Joey talked a lot about Jimmy's family. Joey smelled of beer and Jimmy just answered yes or no when asked a question until the end of the meal when Jimmy asked Sue. "Is there anything I can do to help clean up?"

Tim replied, "You can take out the trash." Which Jimmy did then Joey had Tim show Jimmy to his room. Tim told Jimmy, "I don't like you so stay away from me. You are only here because you can work and we need the extra money."

Jimmy replied, "I understand," then went to his room.

The next morning Joey, Sue, Jr. Joey and Jimmy went to church. They asked Tim if he wanted to go with, but Tim just stayed in bed. On their way home they got KFC chicken and after eating, Joey took Jimmy out to one of the guy's places who had horses for Jimmy to work there. When they got home, Joey said, "Go for a walk with me, Tim."

Tim replied, "Is Sue and little Jr. Joey safe with that, Jimmy? You love them, don't you?"

Joey answered, "More than anything in the world. But I also love you, but I guess guys don't talk about loving one another, so let's change the subject. Jimmy thinks you hate him." Tim motioned yes. "I need you to be half ass nice to Jimmy for Sue. You know how women are. They want us all to get along. So do it." They went back to the house, and Jimmy was playing with Jr. Joey on the floor. Tim just walked over and picked up the baby to put him to bed.

In the morning, Joey walked into Tim's room saying, "You got to get Jimmy set up in school. Here is some money for a lunch ticket and other things he will need. I am not sure if we can trust Jimmy with money." Tim was in full agreement with that.

Jimmy's car was old, and the two boys drove to school without talking. The girls giggled when Jimmy looked back at them. Amy, the High School head cheerleader came up to Tim and said, "Tommy, who is that guy that came to school with you?" She got Tim's name wrong, but then most kids did. Tim didn't answer. Before long the principal was calling Tim to the office about Jimmy and the English Teacher. Tim just called Joey, but Larry answered at work and told Tim, they were on their way. Larry walked in with a box of donuts and Joey went into the office to talk to the principal. Larry sat by Tim after giving the office ladies the donuts. Joey came out; he walked over to Jimmy.

Joey asked Jimmy, "What happened?" Jimmy said nothing. They went back to class, and all was good until the end of the day. Sue's brother started to push Tim around so Jimmy just hit one of them in the stomach and he started to cry. Amy, grab Jimmy's arm and pulled him close to her.

Jimmy took her arm off of him and said, "When you remember Tim's name, then maybe." Tim and Jimmy walked out to his car and just drove home. But this time, Tim looked at Jimmy different, like he was a friend. No one at school pushed Tim around after that; instead, they talked to him.

Weeks later, Sue called Tim aside and said, "Jimmy is having a birthday, and I would like to make him a cake. Ask him what he is doing for his birthday? Is Jimmy going home to his parents?"

Tim did knock on Jimmy's door, and Jimmy said, "Come in." Tim went into Jimmy's room for the first time, and it was very clean. Jimmy sat on his bed playing cards with himself.

Tim said, "Sue wants to know what you are doing for your birthday? Are you going home?"

Jimmy answered, "I am not going back to that place. I don't need anything. I can drive around if that brother of yours lets me have some of my pay for gas. I can find some girls."

Tim reported to Jimmy, "Amy likes you, the red-haired cheerleader at school. She has been nice to me and remembered my name."

Jimmy asked, "Do you want me to go out with her?"

Tim answered, "I don't know. What do you want?"

Jimmy replied, "No, I like blondes. I know most of the time the blondes' hair color comes from a little bottle, but I am okay with that. Peroxide kills the hair color or at least lightens it."

Tim jumped up to say, "My mother was blonde, and it was real."

Jimmy answered, "Yes, your mother was the best. She was like an angel. I always wished she was my mother. I once told her that, and she said we both could be her sons. I'm not lying; it was November 24 at 3 PM. It was a sunny day after Thanksgiving Day."

Tim tried to sound better by saying, "I believe you. My mom was the best, but yours is not bad."

Jimmy looked embarrassed, saying, "Yes, if you like beer bottles hitting you on the head. I am not your cousin; your Uncle George is not my father. Understand Tim? And think about your mother's car accident on the same day Mr. King's wife was shot just like Anna. Maybe your mom saw who shot Mrs. King and Anna was the first one to see your mom after the car accident. Maybe your Mom told Anna something, so they killed her too. Drug dealers in the streets of this small town, this is not New York City. Anna was shot the night Mr. King married Larry's mother, and now Larry has all that money to use."

Tim did not know what to say; he told Sue to make Jimmy a cake. To everyone's surprise, Jimmy's favorite thing was to go to church. Joey worried maybe Jimmy had a crush on Sue, so he asked her one night.

Sue laughed and said, "No it is not me but a thin blonde who goes to church and teaches the little children about God. Jimmy is head over heels in love with her, I can tell.

Jimmy reads her the bible on the phone whenever he can talk to her. I wish I could say it was God but it is just a boy trying to get a girl's attention." Joey just laughed. Jimmy was now going to church three times a week, bible study, teaching children, and a mass. Joey was pleased Jimmy was so easy to handle with the thin blonde around. Jimmy would do anything to see that thin blonde. Joey would give Jimmy some of his pay and Jimmy would buy something for the thin blonde girl who bounced all over when she walked. Tim had also seen a girl at his church who smiled at him. Tim went to church on Saturday, and he liked it that way because they stopped all work on Friday afternoon. Tim had heard his father and Uncle George talk about World War II, but when they saw him, they would always stop talking. Tim had never seen any other family members. He knew his mother came from Germany when she was a young child.

Jimmy's birthday came, and Sue had the boys go to the store and buy a cake mix, frosting, and ice cream, but she was sure to tell Tim to let Jimmy pick out his favorite flavor. They went to the store in Jimmy's car and got chocolate cake with chocolate frosting and vanilla ice cream. Tim wanted to say no chocolate ice cream, but in a flash, Jimmy went. Where did he go so fast and then Tim found Jimmy talking to a thin blonde girl, and he thought it must be this Sylvia from his church. Then a boy came to get her, and she left with her parents in their car. Jimmy could not take his eyes off the girl until the car was out of sight. Home the boys went, and Tim asked Jimmy, "What do you want to do for your birthday?"

Jimmy replied, "After supper with Sue and the family, I would like to go to the movies with Sylvia, you, and a girl for you? Do you think you could get that brother of yours to give me some of my pay for gas and a movie? I already asked Sylvia, but we need another girl."

Tim replied, "I like Betty Edger. She smiles at me in church. Do you know her from school?"

Jimmy answered, "I do know who she is and I will call her for you. You get the money out of Joey." So when Joey walked in the door, Tim went right up to him.

Tim requested, "We want to go to the movies tonight, and Jimmy needs some of his paychecks. Four movie tickets and gas money for the car." Joey looked surprised but Sue motioned "yes."

"Your first date, little brother. Well, you will need money for gas, movie, and maybe pizza after the movie," Joey said handing Tim forty dollars. Jimmy stood off to the side letting Tim know the date was on. After supper and cake with ice cream which Jr. Joey blew out Jimmy's candles. But when Jimmy blew out just one candle would not blow out.

Sue said, "That means Jimmy will have one true love in his life." Tim thought about his birthday, and two candles would not blow out of his cake; would he have two true loves?

They first went to get Betty, and her mother was very nice to Tim. Then Tim took Betty to the car. Jimmy said, "Betty, you and Tim go get Sylvia because her parents will not let her go with a boy but with you two they will." So Tim and Betty went to Sylvia's door, and Betty did all the talking, letting Sylvia's mom know that Tim was her date. To the car they went, and Jimmy could not have been happier. He was a perfect gentleman to Sylvia all night, but when Sylvia found out it was his birthday, she kissed Jimmy on the lips. Tim got his first kiss from Betty.

All was good in the world, Tim had a girlfriend and a best friend. Now no one would mess with him anymore. But as he came home from school one March day he heard Sue crying or maybe it was screaming from Jimmy's bedroom. Tim went in, and Sue was halfway laying on the bed in pain. Tim asked, "What is wrong?"

Sue cried, "The babies are coming now." Jimmy had just come home from work and went to see what was going on. Tim got out the calendar to show Sue it was March, not April.

Jimmy looked at Tim like he had lost his mind and said, "You are at the wrong end, it's not Sue's face where the babies are coming out." Then Jimmy ran out to get help. He got Larry's mom to help them. The first baby came out, and Tim helped support the baby's head. Mrs. King came in to take over and washed up the baby girl. Sue cried in pain again, and Mrs. King handed Jimmy the baby girl. Jimmy held the baby girl close and put her inside his black leather jacket. The baby girl was sucking on Jimmy's little figure when her twin brother was born. Mrs. King wrote on a paper things the boys needed to get from the store which included newborns milk.

Okay, the boys had no money, but they were afraid to tell Mrs. King, so they went to Sue's parents for help, but they would not even answer the door. Then Jimmy went to a bar and found a drunk who he took the money from. Tim asked, "Should we do that?"

Jimmy replied, "He is just going to drink it all up anyway. He is already drunk, so he will not miss it. The babies need milk." So, to the store, they went to get baby supplies. Jimmy was sure he knew nothing about diapers, but he did read the boxes and home they went with the stuff. A good night sleep was not easy because the babies needed to feed a lot, it felt like every hour on the hour. Sue was too weak, so the boys did their best. Mrs. King did stay the night and showed the boys how to feed the babies.

In the morning, they set out to find Joey. Mrs. King called her son, Larry, and he told her where Joey was, not at work but a motel. Jimmy was mad, and Tim followed him to the car. At the motel, Jimmy kicked in the door, and there was Joey with some woman in bed. The woman grabbed her clothes and ran.

Joey tried to explain, but Jimmy took Joey's clothes and ran them up that flagpole. Jimmy and Tim went to the car, with Joey crying, "Come on."

Tim said to Jimmy. "I am glad you came to live with us. You are my best friend."

Jimmy replied, "I would not have missed this for the world. I am glad to be here. You are the only true friend I have ever had." Jimmy and Tim did not tell Sue. But was it for

Joey or did they not want to hurt Sue? They had three babies in the house which kept everyone busy. Joey was extra nice to the boys, being afraid they would tell Sue where he was when his twins were born. Then Joey and Sue got married in the church Jimmy always went to with Sylvia. Joey was now twenty-one years old and could marry. It was a small wedding, just them and Jimmy and Tim's girlfriends. Sylvia was now able to work with Sue, taking care of the babies. Sylvia's parents let her work there for pay and Jimmy could see Sylvia all the time. All was good. What could go wrong?

One sunny afternoon, Jimmy knocked on Tim's bedroom door. Tim answered, "Yes, Jimmy, come in." They were alone that afternoon; Sue had taken the kids to the doctor for checkups. Joey was never home much. There was nothing that could have prepared Tim for what Jimmy was going to say. Believe it or not.

Jimmy said, "Tim, look what is coming out of my head. It is silver and looks like horns, but it is in the middle of my skull. Am I crazy? Just look, Tim."

Tim got up and looked at these silver things like an antenna for a car or something on the top of Jimmy's head. Tim studied them for a minute and was waiting for Jimmy to laugh or something, it was a joke right? But no one was laughing, so Tim touched them.

Jimmy pulled away saying, "That hurt. Please tell no one. Not even Sylvia. She may not love me anymore. I am a freak."

For the summer, the boys tried to find out what was on Jimmy's head but it came from the inside out, and it was silver. Jimmy reported dreams of a place underground with white-haired people. Jimmy admitted he had these types of dreams ever since he could remember. But he had never seen the silver things before. They went to the library and looked in medical books, but then in Larry's office, they found something about a government group called the Majestic Twelve on UFO's which Larry was on.

Tim was a senior in high school, and so was Jimmy. Jimmy was very smart and could pass grades ahead. They also took college classes. Tim wanted to be a doctor. Jimmy just wanted a good job so he could marry Sylvia. Time passed, Halloween, Thanksgiving, Christmas, Valentines Day, and Easter with their girlfriends was fun. Jimmy and Tim graduated from high school with honors. But how to pay for college?

Jimmy's friends Kenny and Eddie had the answer, to rob a bank with Eddie's Dad. Jimmy had said no to this, but Tim talked him into it, to be the driver in the getaway car. It would be money for college and Jimmy to marry his Sylvia. Well, everything went wrong, and Eddie's dad shot a guard. To the car, they ran, and Jimmy drove them away fast, then he would burn the car.

Jimmy noticed in the back seat a bag of money Eddie's dad forgot and the gun. Jimmy removed them and then burned the car. He went home to tell Tim all about it. It was all over the news, and then Larry came to Tim's home all upset. But it was not about the robbery. Larry needed Jimmy to go and help Joey someplace they were not supposed to be. Larry said, "Joey is hurt, and two guys got killed. It is all my fault. I need Jimmy to go and give Joey blood so we can move them home. I have to get them out of there and fast."

Tim saw this as a way out for Jimmy with the bank robbery, so Tim made a deal with Larry. If Larry got the boys off and just blamed Eddie's dad, then Jimmy would go and help Joey. Larry agreed, but he needed the gun which Tim got from Jimmy. Larry and his lawyer went with the boys to the police. Tim was the hero for finding the bank robber, and the boys got left out of it. But not all the money was ever found. Eddie's Dad went to jail for it.

Jimmy went with Larry after talking it over with Sylvia and Tim promised to see Sylvia every day for Jimmy. Sylvia still helped Sue with the babies, and Tim picked her up in Jimmy's car.

They were gone almost a month, but then one night, Joey and Jimmy walked through Tim's front door. Jimmy called Sylvia. They fell asleep on the phone and Tim hung up the phone for Jimmy. But Jimmy never told Tim what had happened. Tim had other problems, Betty was pregnant, and Tim had to have Joey find their dad to sign for him to marry Betty. Joey said, "No you are too young. That baby is her problem. I will not have you throw away your life on this mistake. You stay in school and be that doctor you want to be."

Tim was broken hearted. Betty's parents agreed that they should just get married. Sue asked Tim, "What do you want to do?"

Tim answered, "I want to marry Betty and have this family."

Sue then went to Jimmy for help. Jimmy thought for a minute and then said, "Okay, let's find your dad. I bet he is with his brother George in the bar in my hometown." Out the door they went with Joey right behind them.

They drove to the bar and there they were, sitting in the bar drunk. Tim went to talk to his dad. Uncle George called, "Who is paying for our bar bill?" Joey went up to the barmaid and paid the bill but also gave her his phone number. Now was that to call him if there was more of a bill or was it something else? Maybe to get together later, but Jimmy said nothing about it. Tim took his dad home, but he slept most of the time.

Tim and Betty's wedding plans started. How was Tim to know this would be the last time he would see his father? Everyone had a great time at Tim and Betty's wedding. The whole town came, and it was all outside. A big spring wedding with flowers everywhere. Larry gave Tim a job at his company and would pay for him to go to college as he worked. Jimmy even got down on one knee with a diamond and said, "Will you marry me? I love you so much. Please marry me?"

Sylvia was crying, and she said, "Yes oh, yes. I love you too." Sylvia put the ring on a chain around her neck so no one could see it. Only Tim and Betty knew. But from that day on, Jimmy planned their wedding. First, he got Sylvia's wedding dress with ruffles on the back, long and white. Jimmy planned for them to run away and get married that June.

Things were great for Tim. They lived with Betty's parents, but Tim was with Jimmy most of the time until the baby was born. Tim's baby boy was born sick with the same health issues he had. Tim went in to tell his wife, Betty about his failure. "Our son, Merit, is sick like me," Tim said.

Betty looked up at Tim with her green eyes and replied, "Don't worry so. I know you and Jimmy will find a cure. You can do anything. I love you." Tim walked out of that room feeling like he could do anything but going to college was harder than he knew. It was hard even with Jimmy's help. So Jimmy went to Gerald Dogenmeier, the company doctor, for him to help Tim. Gerald did not like Tim, but Jimmy knew Gerald needed money to pay back taxes on his parents' home that he lived in so Jimmy gave Gerald some of the robbery money to pay his taxes and Gerald helped Tim. Gerald would also help Tim with his son's health issues.

Tim did like his job at Larry's company, and now college was easier. But Tim wanted to live in his parents' home with his wife and son. Jimmy was to also stay, but the house was not big enough for all of them, so Tim talked to Jimmy about the problem.

Jimmy said, "Let's get Sue and the kids a place in the country. I know that is what Sue wants. I still have some of that bank money. No one will notice, they will think it is from Joey and your paychecks."

So the boys looked in the newspaper and found the perfect place. They found a place not far from town, the right amount of rooms and the price was good. They bought it without looking at it first. They paid cash and drove out with Sue to show her the place. What a mess. Now, I don't know if you had ever seen this old TV show called Green Acres. It is about a city lawyer who buys a farm where nothing works.

When they opened the door, it fell off. When they walked in, the floor fell in. Dark water came from the sink. A sound came when they turned on the lights. But Sue loved it. The two city boys looked at each other, what had they done? Sue did agree it needed a little work. The money that went into fixing it up would have cost less just to have started all over again, but they didn't because Sue loved it. Sue stayed with them until the work was completed. The guys worked overtime and they paid for it.

At last, it was time for Jimmy and Sylvia to run away and get married. Tim did not see them before they left because he had to work. Merit got sick, and Tim had to take him to the doctor. Betty, Tim's wife, had taken his car, so Tim used Jimmy's car to find Gerald the doctor for Merit. Tim wondered where Jimmy and Sylvia went without a car? But he continued to drive around looking for Gerald and finally, did find him in a bar, drunk. Tim used coffee to help Gerald sober up, and in time, Gerald was able to help Merit.

After Tim put Merit to sleep, he sat down by the TV to watch anything. He would put gas in Jimmy's car in a minute for he had used most of it to find Gerald. As Tim watched TV, he saw a bad train accident that hit a car on the railroad tracks. The car looked like

Jimmy's. Tim ran to his neighbor to ask if he would watch Merit. Then Tim ran down to the railroad tracks where the accident happened. Jimmy was lying there on the ground as the ambulance came to take him to the hospital. Tim ran up to him.

Jimmy said, "Find Sylvia, the car stopped on the railroad tracks and the train was coming. I got her out, but she went running back to the car for something, and then the train hit the car. I found Sylvia, I held her close, and we kissed, but then everything went black." I think there is a song like that but who knows. Was Jimmy thinking correct?

Larry came over to Tim and said, "Let me give you a ride to the hospital so you can be with Jimmy."

Tim replied, "We need to find Sylvia for Jimmy." They looked but couldn't find her.

Larry said after some time looking for Sylvia, "Maybe Sylvia went in another ambulance to the hospital. Let's go, Jimmy needs you. We can't trust all those doctors." So at the hospital, they went to find Jimmy. Tim called Sue from the hospital as Larry tried to find out anything about the accident. Sue got there and sat with Tim, which felt like forever waiting. Larry came back saying, "The police report has only Jimmy with the car. No Sylvia. Are you sure she was with him? Jimmy was hurt and could be mistaken."

Jimmy got out in a few days and Tim took him home, but Jimmy was sure Sylvia was with him. Jimmy could not sleep or eat until he could find his Sylvia. They did find the wedding dress in the car, and it was out of the wrapped box. Did Sylvia wear the wedding dress the night before as planned but where did they go without a car? Larry got a lawyer for Jimmy, and he didn't even get a traffic ticket. But still no Sylvia. Next they went to her home, but no one lived there. The neighbors said a young couple with two small children had lived there, but they moved a few weeks ago. Tim was sure he talked to Sylvia's mother there with Betty on their first date. Then he had picked up Sylvia many times there, but he never went into the house. Sylvia had a brother, a little younger than her who lived there. Tim was sure of this but no more. Sue called Sylvia's phone number which was not working.

They spent the summer looking for Sylvia with no luck. No one had seen her with Jimmy that day or the night before. Not even Tim had seen them together. Had Sylvia broke up with Jimmy as in the song she loved so much, The Leader of The Pack? Tim didn't know, but the song was about a girl whose parents do not like the guy she is dating and she has to break up with him, so he drives into traffic without knowing what happens to him. That song went over and over in Tim's mind as they looked for Sylvia.

School started. Tim went back to working and college. What would Jimmy do? Jimmy did a lot of praying for his Sylvia, then came the answer to his prayer. Kenny and Eddie were going off to spy school. They were both going to be agents for the government. Jimmy just said, "No."

Tim thought fast and started to talk Jimmy into it by saying, "We need more skills to find Sylvia. We are just not finding her. You would learn how to find someone and maybe get into files on people." That was all it took, and Jimmy was off to spy school with Kenny, and Eddie. Tim could hardly wait for Jimmy to come home and he did, for Halloween, Thanksgiving, Christmas, Easter, and then the summer. They wrote lots of letters and made phone calls, but they were all about finding Sylvia. Larry and the guys did not think this was healthy for Jimmy. Even Gerald, who was a friend to Jimmy, thought a summer job might help Jimmy take his mind off Sylvia. Charles, one of the guys who worked for Larry, had the answer. His mother needed help working on their family farm. There was not much to do because the land was in a government program not to plant for seven years, but the place needed upkeep. There would be fresh air and little hands-on work to repair things around the farm.

They talked to Jimmy, and he said, "No."

But Tim talked to Jimmy and said, "Sylvia's parents know you are looking for her. So if you take this job, maybe they'll think you have moved on, and we can find a clue as to where they have taken her." Jimmy agreed and went to work for Charles' mother on their farm for the summer. They still looked for Sylvia, and that was still all Jimmy talked about, but some nights he did not come home. Tim thought nothing of it until one Saturday morning, Jimmy came home and went right to his room. Charles, Jim, and Joey were right behind him. What was going on?

Charles cried, "Why Jimmy?" Jimmy did not reply. The story turned out to be very interesting. Tim found out that Jimmy was in bed with Charles' mother. Was this a slip from The Graduate in that movie where a guy sleeps with someone's mother? Charles' mother was a widow and a very pretty blonde. Tim did not know what to think, so he called Larry. Larry came laughing and had Charles send his mother to live in Paris, France and Jimmy just went back to college. No one said any more about it, but the whole town knew and was whispering about it.

Jimmy came home on Halloween and all he wanted to do was look for Sylvia. They started looking at grave sites which were a little spooky. At an old run down castle, they heard a woman crying. Jimmy ran to find her and Tim followed. By the time Tim got there, Jimmy had already seen her face, and it was not Sylvia. But who was it and why was she alone here?

Jimmy just walked away, and Tim tried to talk with the woman. It turned out to be Larry's wife who lived in his mother's old run down castle alone. Larry had his two children with his mother at Mr. King's house, his stepfather. Tim took the woman named Linda, straight to Mr. King's house and talked to Larry's mother, who called Larry. Mrs. King cleaned up Linda and had words with Larry on how to treat his wife. Mr. King also talked in a low voice to Larry.

Larry said how sorry he was and that he needed Tim to help him get his wife, Linda to be more ladylike for a man of his position. Jimmy knew this was a very bad idea. But Tim agreed for he needed the extra money it would pay. Tim promised Jimmy he would never sleep with Larry's wife. Jimmy just shook his head no. Linda turned out to be a handful and was no lady. She was mean to Tim and dressed all wrong. Betty and Linda did become good friends; this helped Tim. Jimmy just went back to school.

Thanksgiving came, and Jimmy got out of school a few days sooner, so he came straight home to Tim to work on finding Sylvia. Jimmy walked into Tim's home to find Tim's wife Betty in bed with another man. Jimmy just left and drove to Tim's office saying, "Come with me now." Tim took his son, Merit, and followed Jimmy. They drove to Tim's house and walked in to find Betty sleeping in Tim's bed with this other guy. Tim just turned and walked out of the house, Jimmy followed with Merit. They drove around until the guy's car was gone, then they went home. But Tim said nothing about it to his wife, Betty. Jimmy threw up in the bathroom.

In the morning, Tim asked Jimmy, "Is there a place we could send this guy? He works for Larry, and I am in charge of personnel at the company." Jimmy found a place in South America and Larry signed the paper with all his other papers Tim gave him to sign, without reading it. The guy was never heard from again; no one even missed him.

Yes, Tim's wife was pregnant. Tim sent her to Paris, France. Jimmy did not understand, but they had more time to look for Sylvia. Tim did keep his son, Merit, with him. And Jimmy went back to college but before he left, Jimmy told Tim about having a relationship with his boss's wife and all the problems that would bring him.

Jimmy said, "Two wrongs don't make this right." Tim promised Jimmy he would never do that. Jimmy said no more for he did not want Tim to remind him of his relationship with Charles' mother that last summer. They still had no luck finding Sylvia dead or alive. Easter came and then the anniversary of that car accident with Jimmy only being sadder. Jimmy was very moody and hard to be around, so Tim took his vacation to help Jimmy look for Sylvia. Joey and Sue were worried about Jimmy.

Joey told Tim, "Have Jimmy get some help, to go see some doctor. Do they want a spy with issues?"

Well, it turned out yes they do. Tim said, "Jimmy's anger issues helped make him a better hitman." Tim was joking, but the whole town now believed Jimmy was a hitman for the government but which government was it? Jimmy went through his college as he did high school. Jimmy was a genius, but no one had noticed because of his issues over Sylvia.

Tim sent Betty's parents to live with her in Paris because Betty had the baby and it was a girl. The sad part was the baby girl also had Tim's health issues, so he knew it was his daughter. Gerald and Tim were the doctors who tried to help Jimmy with his issue, which was finding Sylvia. Tim did not have to go to medical school to know that was the only problem Jimmy had.

CHAPTER TWO

MARGO ELGIN, THEY SENT ME AWAY AND I LOVE THEM

It was a cold January morning and Margo did not want to go to school. Margo was sure all she had to do was look sad and Uncle Tim and Jimmy would let her stay home. Margo loved to stay at Uncle Jimmy's home even if his housekeeper and her husband were always there with them. Sometimes the boys stayed too, Jr. Joey, Merit, and Mark, her twin brother. Jimmy was Margo's Godfather at church and he got her anything she wanted. Margo always remembered the story of how Jimmy held her in his black leather jacket to keep her warm the day she was born, and she sucked on his little figure because that is what babies do.

Sue called to Margo, "Hurry up, the boys are ready for school. You'll miss the school bus." But Margo stayed in bed. Sue continued to call, "Let's not start this again, or I will hit you and hard."

Margo was now going to show Sue, her mother, who was boss. Margo went to her new princess phone and called Uncle Tim's house. Jimmy answered the phone, "Hello!" Margo just loved his voice.

Margo cried, "Uncle Jimmy, Mommy is going to hit me hard."

"Your Uncle Tim and I will be right there. Let me talk to your mommy." Jimmy said he was upset. Sue did not say much to Jimmy on the phone but if looks could kill, sweet little Margo would have been dead. The boys left on the school bus as Tim and Jimmy came to their house.

Tim said, "What is this I hear, Margo is not going to school today?"

"Maybe she is sick. Margo is just a sweet little girl," Jimmy said as Margo ran out to climb on his lap. Jimmy gave Margo a new stuff animal and wiped her tears away. Tim and Sue talked in the kitchen, but Margo did not have to go to school that day. Sue took the baby who was born sick to the doctor. Margo went to work with Uncle Tim and Jimmy, then out to lunch and shopping for more toys.

When Sue got home and heard all the fun Margo had and saw the new toys, Sue said, "You two spoil Margo so much she thinks she can do anything she wants." Neither Jimmy nor Tim disagreed with Sue but they continued to spoil Margo. That night, after the guys left, Margo, heard a noise.

Sue whispered, "Margo, call your Uncles on your princess phone then hide in that secret place they taught you until you hear their voices. Don't talk, be very quiet." Margo called them.

Jimmy answered the phone, "Hello!"

Margo said, "Mommy told me to call you to come out here right away and then to hide, okay."

Jimmy replied, "We are on our way. Hide until I tell you it is safe to come out." Within minutes Margo was sure she heard Jimmy fighting with someone. Then later, she heard Uncle Tim talking with her mom who was crying. Margo did not come out of her special hiding place until she heard Jimmy say, "Margo, please come out now, it is safe. Tim and I are here." Margo ran out to Jimmy's arms and he held her close to him. After that night, the kids had to go to private schools. The boys went to a military school and Margo to a church boarding school for girls. Tim was never sure who cried more about it, Margo or Jimmy. But the kids had to be kept safe.

Each morning, Jimmy and Margo had breakfast at the school then went to church with the Sisters. Tim waited in the car with his coffee. Jimmy called Margo each night to say her prayers on the phone. Tim just went to sleep. And somehow Merit found his way to bed. Things were going well. Joey was in rehab for drugs and it was a drug dealer who wanted money from Joey or he would hurt Joey's family. Jimmy had taken down these drug dealers but there was always someone new selling drugs. Sue was in the hospital a lot with the new baby. Jimmy was gone a lot at night, was he working or what? Tim was not sure but he had a major problem as Sue told him Linda, Larry's wife, was pregnant and Joey could not understand how this could happen. Larry was gone with government work for contract all the time. Tim just passed out on the floor.

Sue cried, "Someone call Jimmy." Gerald tried, but Jimmy's housekeeper told him Jimmy does not sleep there at night. So Gerald put Tim in the hospital and waited for Jimmy to come to Tim's house to call Margo for prayers. Jimmy always left right after prayers with Margo, but where did he go? Did Jimmy have a girlfriend?'

Jimmy walked into Tim's house to call Margo and Gerald was waiting. Jimmy said, "What is up?" Then he called Margo and did the prayers with her as he waited for Gerald to talk.

Gerald said as Jimmy got off the phone, "Tim is in the hospital. Tim fell as Sue was talking to him. Got a girlfriend? What is your girlfriend's name? Do I know her?"

Jimmy did not answer Gerald. He just left for the hospital with Gerald following him still asking questions about Jimmy having a girlfriend. They went to the hospital and Jimmy went right to see Tim. Tim was now awake, but he looked very bad. Tim was so white in his face, one could think he died. Jimmy asked, "What happened?"

Tim replied, "Sue told me Linda is pregnant. What am I going to do? My illness? Do you think Larry, my boss, would be upset about me getting his wife pregnant? I have not always been going to work but pay myself and I have been taking some of his money for my needs." Jimmy just looked out the window, and Gerald laughed. No one else was in the room to hear this.

Gerald said, "Tim, I think Jimmy has a girlfriend. If a guy is gone at night only then comes home in the morning!" Jimmy just looked at Gerald as if looks could kill, Gerald would die. Tim was looking better and sat up.

Tim replied, "Jimmy, I think we should talk about the woman you are seeing? It is about time. Sylvia has been gone how many years now? And I never saw you and her go in that car. Also, how did you two run away when I had your car? Did you maybe forget and you were alone in the car when that train hit? Did Sylvia break up with you because her parents made her and then took her away? Did they find out Sylvia was working with Sue and that you were there? I know Sylvia's parents did not like you. Or did Sylvia have another boyfriend?"

Jimmy looked at Tim like he was crazy. "Tim, what are you talking about? You think I would hurt Sylvia? I loved her. But now you want me to help you? Tim, this is not a way to ask for help." Jimmy looked down and continued, "Her name is Marci. We work together with this group. I want to get married and have a family. I think, Tim, we could do a blood transfusion on the baby when it is born with no issues for the child. You always deliver the babies for the employees at the company so we could do it easily. It would be better for the baby. How much money did you take?"

Tim replied like he was afraid of Jimmy, "I am not sure, a few million." Gerald laughed out loud.

Jimmy's eyes opened wide, but Sue walked in, so Jimmy said nothing. Sue said, "How is Tim doing? There is an issue at Margo's school, should I go?"

"No, we can do it. Tim will be just fine. Gerald can give him something. Right Gerald?" Jimmy said. Gerald nodded yes. Sue went out with the baby. Jimmy and Tim left for Margo's school.

At the school, Margo had hit another little girl, and the girl's tooth fell out. Tim looked at Jimmy. Jimmy said, "Give this money to the head Sister, and I will talk to Margo. I am sure it was not her fault. Children lose their teeth at this age anyway."

Tim replied, "I am sure the other little girl with the bloody mouth had it coming. Margo does not have a mark on her. How do I know who is the head Sister, they all look like a penguin."

"The one with the ruler and looks the maddest. Here is a little more money. We have a situation where throwing more money at it, will make it go away." Jimmy said as he took little Margo to her dorm room and sat on her bed. Then Jimmy said to Margo, "I thought we did your prayers and you were going to sleep. What happened?" Margo said nothing with her lower lip out. Then Jimmy tugged Margo into bed and kissed her goodnight on the forehead saying, "I'll see you for breakfast and church. Maybe you will feel like talking more in the morning." Margo shook her head no and Jimmy left the room. Jimmy smiled at a Sister that Tim gave a great deal of money to, maybe for the dentist for the other little girl. They left the school.

Tim asked, "Now tell me about your new girlfriend." Jimmy replied, "Tim, I have to go, I promised her I would be back tonight." Jimmy just dropped Tim at home and left. But in the morning Jimmy was at the school having breakfast with Margo and church. Tim waited in the car with his coffee. He didn't want to talk to any more Sisters.

Sue was waiting when they came. Tim said, "I think Sue wants to know about your girlfriend?"

Jimmy replied, "More than likely she wants to know about her daughter, Margo." But Jimmy was wrong. Sue wanted to know all about Jimmy's new girlfriend. Jimmy said very little but, "I have known her for three months and her name is Marci."

"Can we meet her? Sunday after church for lunch at my home? Does she go to church with you? What faith is she? What does Marci like to eat?" Sue asked. Tim was laughing.

Jimmy didn't know what to say, so he just nodded okay, but then he said, "Marci' does not eat meat. She dresses a little different and has a whip. I don't like her whip. Marci lived with her grandmother and is blonde. Marci's grandmother just died so be nice to her. Marci is a very nice person and is very smart. She smells nice."

Tim looked at Sue, and she looked at Tim like Jimmy is really into this Marci. From that time on, everything was about the lunch that Sunday. Joey was so interested in meeting Jimmy's new girlfriend, and all the guys wanted to know how she looked. Then, what about this whip? Does Marci use the whip on Jimmy and why does he not like it? Tim stayed close to Jimmy, and after prayers, Jimmy was leaving to be with Marci so Tim said, "Can I go? Merit is with Sue. I feel a little sick and should not be alone tonight. I don't want to go back to the hospital."

Jimmy was not pleased but said, "Okay, get in the car but watch what you say and be nice." To a big house, they went, and Jimmy talked to a very pretty girl standing by a desk with her legs apart working on some papers. She did have a nice ass as she bent over the desk.

Jimmy said, "Tim this is Marci. Marci, this is Tim, my friend I have told you about, who I stay with a lot."

Marci smiled and said, "Jimmy has talked a lot about you. You're Margo's uncle." Tim nodded yes, but he couldn't say anymore because Jimmy had never spoken of Marci until today. This house is big and full with people without homes. Tim slept in a chair that folded out into a bed. Jimmy slept with Marci on a black leather bed chair thing. Tim was listening all night long, but did not hear any sex, but they did talk very low. Jimmy slept better than he had in years.

Sunday came, and all the kids were home with Joey looking out the window. Tim and Merit had just come, and now Jimmy came in with Marci. She was tall with long blonde hair, very pretty. Marci had a nice blue dress. Jimmy introduced her to everyone. Margo looked mad, but Marci whispered to Margo, "Jimmy and I are just friends, we work together to help our people, you and Sylvia are his true loves." Margo watched them closely, and Jimmy put Margo between them.

Then, after prayers, one of the boys asked Marci to pass the chicken, so she picked up a chicken leg and threw it at him. The other boys asked Marci to pass them something, and she did the same. Hands full of potatoes went flying across the table. Was this a little much for Sue? No one said a word about it, not even Jimmy. He just ate like there was nothing wrong with it.

After the meal, Marci asked, "Can I help clean up?" Sue just nodded yes, food was all over the place. Jimmy read Margo a bible story. Tim and Joey watch TV. The boys helped Marci clean up the floor.

Sue started to talk to Marci and said "Do you like to cook? What kind of work do you and Jimmy do together? Where do you live? In your grandma's home? Sorry, she died."

Marci answered very nicely, "I don't know how to cook. Maybe you could teach me how to make a few of Jimmy's favorite dishes. We live together to help people where I live because they are very poor. Jimmy got me this new dress today. Jimmy does not want me to stay at my grandmother's old house. He wants me to live with him at his home where we are at."

Sue stood there with her mouth open, but nothing came out. So Marci went out to Jimmy. Jimmy looked up and said, "Are we ready to go, Marci?"

Marci replied, "Could we take Margo with us so she can pick out a room at your home? Would you like to go with us, Margo?" Margo smiled yes, and Jimmy looked at Sue who looked at Joey who just got off the phone and was running to the bathroom.

Sue said, "Okay, but Tim, you go with them. I'll watch Merit for you." And off they went.

In the car, Jimmy said, "I think that went very good. What do you think Margo?" Tim just put his finger to his lips to not answer. Marci looked pleased. When they got back to that place, Marci showed Margo the house and the work they were doing in the house included a bedroom for Margo. Jimmy said, "I want you to stay here with me a lot and Marci."

For supper, Jimmy took Margo and Tim out to eat on their way back to Margo's school. Jimmy did the prayers with Margo and then gave Margo Marci's phone number. Margo asked, "Why do I need Marci's phone number?"

Jimmy replied, "Maybe you want to talk with another girl who's not your mom. So you can call Marci anytime. What if you can't get me on the phone or Uncle Tim. Just call Marci for anything you may need. She will always help you." Margo was still not so sure of this Marci.

Tim could hardly wait to get Jimmy alone and then he just said, "Marci is a little different than I thought she would be. Why does she throw food? Where was her whip?"

Jimmy replied as he dropped Tim off at home, "Marci is different than anyone I have ever known. I like her too. She has her whip at night. Does she throw food? I didn't notice." Jimmy left for Marci's or his new home wherever it was. Tim didn't know about this place. Tim came in to see Sue and Joey waiting for him.

Sue said, "Did you tell Jimmy about throwing food? Does she eat with her hands? Is Jimmy going to marry her? They live together."

Tim answered, "I will talk to Jimmy more in the morning. He is not here now but with Marci. Jimmy sleeps very well with her. You know Jimmy's had trouble sleeping since Sylvia is gone."

In the morning, Jimmy came for Tim to go see Margo and Tim said, "Did you notice Marci eats with her figures? She doesn't use silverware. Are you planning to marry her?"

Jimmy looked annoyed. "What is it you don't like about her, because they are poor? What is wrong with using your fingers to eat? Why are we so perfect? Well, if you don't like Marci, then I guess you don't like me either. I don't know where this relationship is going, but I like her. I want to get married and have a family before I am old. Maybe I am not good enough for her. Did you ever think of that?" Jimmy got out of the car and slammed the door.

Tim answered quickly out the window, "No, I like her too. I eat with my fingers too sometimes, maybe I should. I am a poor person too." Jimmy went into the church, and Tim stayed in the car. As soon as Tim got back he called Sue and told her not to question Jimmy about Marci; it was serious.

After that, no one asked Jimmy about Marci and Jimmy went to see Marci every night. But in the morning he would come back to have breakfast and church with Margo. Jimmy said to Tim one day, "Could you follow me to Marci's; I just bought her this car. Oh, that is okay, I will have Marci drive me home in the morning. She does need the practice driving."

Tim just called Sue to tell her all about the car Jimmy bought for Marci. In the morning the school called before Jimmy came and Margo was in trouble again. Tim called Jimmy and Marci answered the phone. She did not say anything but gave the phone to Jimmy. He was very close to her. Still in bed, Tim guessed. Tim said, "Margo's school called, and our little angel is in trouble again. Can you come soon?"

19

Jimmy replied, "We are late. Please go to my room and get some money out of the top drawer. Bring all of the money. I will have Marci drop me off at your place."

Tim waited, and they were there in twenty minutes, so where did this Marci live. They did not kiss as Jimmy got out of the car and into Tim's car. To the church, they went. Margo had peed in the Holy water dish. Tim gave the head Sister money, and Jimmy talked to Margo. Jimmy asked, "What happened?"

Margo said, "I had to pee, and the Sister told me to be quiet. I peed in the dish with the water like a toilet. Where were you, I had to eat my breakfast alone?" Jimmy just looked down. All settled down, and Jimmy showed Margo where the restrooms were in the church. But Tim knew Margo did know where the bathroom was and she did it just because Jimmy was not there for breakfast with her. No more was ever said about it again.

Joey was out of rehab and school was almost over. Margo got upset because Sue would not let her stay with Jimmy and Marci for the weekend. Margo cried all weekend to Jimmy about it.

That Monday, Margo put crazy glue on a cross, their Sister kissed it and got the glue on her mouth. Tim called Jimmy. They took money, but they threw it at the head Sister and ran with little Margo out of the school, leaving her things. They did not look back, but kept moving.

Tim and Margo stayed with Jimmy and Marci for the weekend. Margo slept with Jimmy and Marci, but Jimmy had Marci in the middle of them. Tim slept in his chair bed which was nice.

Summer came, and Linda had her baby with a blood transfusion. Work was so busy at the company that Larry never noticed. Larry's company needed a contract with the government for guys to have work. Jimmy was back to work as a spy. Tim tried to see Jimmy, but the only place Margo and Tim found Jimmy was with Marci. Sue did let Margo stay with Marci a lot over that summer. Jimmy had the people from the area stay at his house as their home got repaired. Tim was still confused about where this place was and why he could not find it without Jimmy programming it into his car to drive him there. Sue did meet with Marci to help her learn to cook, but Marci was sure she was not Jimmy's girlfriend. Margo agreed they did not kiss, or Jimmy did not touch Marci like a girlfriend, but they did sleep together, and Margo slept with them too. Nothing was going on between Jimmy and Marci.

When school, started, the kids went to a private school, even Merit. Margo went to a princess school which she loved. Jimmy worked a lot, and Tim was busy trying to help Larry's business work. Tim promised Jimmy he would stop sleeping with Larry's wife and put the money back.

Jimmy came home for Halloween to take the kids trick or treating. Jimmy got truckloads of pumpkins for Marci and the people to crave the pumpkins into Jack-O-lanterns for

Halloween. They would eat the insides of the pumpkins on Thanksgiving as none of them ate meat. The head Sister of Margo's old school sent Margo's things from the school that they had left and a Halloween costume of an angel with a crooked halo. Tim laughed so hard and called Jimmy, saying, "You must come here, the penguin lady, that Sister is human and funny. She sent Margo an angel outfit with a crooked halo." Jimmy and Marci came right away and laughed.

That night Jimmy and Tim took the kids trick or treating but after a few homes Jimmy said, "I have to go." He left in a flash. The boys teased Jimmy had a girlfriend Marci, and they made kissing sounds. Margo cried. Tim continued the trick or treating until the kids were too much for him, so he took them to Sue and promised Margo he would find Jimmy. Tim called Marci, but there was no answer. Tim's car did not take him to them. Where was this place?

Tim did not see Jimmy until Thanksgiving when he walked into Tim's house. Tim said, "Where have you been? You have not called me or anything since Halloween. What happened?"

Jimmy replied, "I have talked to Margo each day. She is growing up so fast. She likes boys now. Maybe the kids should come home to live and go to public school. Margo needs her mother." Tim wanted to argue with Jimmy on this, but there were so many problems at work that Larry had asked if Jimmy could help somehow. Tim was sure Jimmy would never agree to it.

Thanksgiving didn't go well that year because they had a different pastor and he had people bring food to be blessed, but they did not know that. Tim thought the food at the church was to eat and so he ate it. The women at the church started to scream and run up to get their food. Jimmy grabbed a chair to hold off the women as they tried to hit them with their handbags. The pastor looked mad. Jimmy threw Tim the keys to the car and as on the old TV show the Dukes of Hazard, they jumped into the car, but the women followed them. Jimmy lost the women in their cars at the trees because he was driving very fast to get away from those angry women. Tim was limping as he fell down the stairs at the church on his way to the car from their getaway. They were now safe at Sue's, but she was not happy with them.

Sue asked, "What did you guys do in church this morning? I have to see these women all the time." Joey and the boys came out laughing. Sue explained to them that on Thanksgiving people bring their favorite dish and the pastor blesses it, and then they take it home to eat. They would have to make this up to those women and be nice.

Tim said, "I will take them flowers and tell them that their food was irresistible. I will tell the ladies how sorry we are. Jimmy can help pay for all the flowers I will need." Jimmy nodded in agreement. Sue went and got a list of names for Tim to give flowers.

Joey said, "I am not letting my kids go to public school. I want them gone. Understand me?"

Jimmy just answered, "I am not paying for private schools anymore. You can pay for it." No one said another word about it, but the kids went to public schools after that.

Margo took Jimmy aside and whispered in his ear, "Uncle Tim needs your help with his boss's company or Daddy, and he may not have a job. Please help them. Thanks for public school."

The next day, Jimmy was at Tim's office looking through paperwork, trying to find out where Larry was in trouble. After a few weeks, Jimmy said, "Larry needs a government contract and a group to help him stay out of trouble. The contract will put the guys to work, but the group will cost Larry some money." Tim agreed, and things started moving along.

Jimmy stayed over Christmas and started the group. Tim did not know any of these new people, there were men and women, old and young people. Marci was one of the six women on the team. Jimmy paired up men with women about the same age. Tim was to be the treasurer to get money from Larry. But the cost was very little, just paper and lunch. They always met in the boardroom at Larry's company. Jimmy was the president and a woman named Venus was his secretary, being Jimmy's partner which Marci did not like. Jimmy paired Marci up with a rich guy about her age named George; he liked Marci. Was this a good idea for Jimmy to do? Tim asked.

Jimmy answered, but Tim couldn't say anything. "I am the president of the group, Neal is the vice president, Venus is the secretary, and you are the treasurer. Marci and George are security; Sandy is the record clerk, Carla is your partner and the bookkeeper, Paula and Victor are the scouts, Jack and Unisa are the advisers. So what is it that you need to know?"

"I want to talk with Neal, the vice president. I want to be sure you are safe. What do we do for Larry?" Tim asked. Jimmy just gave Tim Neal's phone number and left. Tim called Neal right away and made the meeting and said, "Jimmy does not appear to be upset about Marci and George. What do you think? Isn't Marci Jimmy's girlfriend?"

Neal smiled and said, "Jimmy and I are good friends, so we do not talk about women. But Jimmy did bring a picture with him when I first got to know him. It was a blonde-haired woman, and he asked me if I knew her and I said yes. I took Jimmy to see her, and it was Venus. She was in a light cloth dress that you could see the shape of her body. Then next thing I know, Venus is in the group Jimmy started for your boss, Larry. Maybe Jimmy is interested in Venus because he made her his partner and he does spend a lot of time with her. The very late night he's working on notes for the meeting, Jimmy forgets to go home."

Tim said, "What else do you know about this Venus? Is she nice? Is she married? What is her family? Where do they live?"

"I am not saying anymore but she is very, and I mean very rich. I have heard they eat on gold dishes," Neal said, but then he just left Tim sitting there thinking. Tim then went to tell Sue.

Tim asked Jimmy the minute he came home, "Are you seeing this Venus, the rich woman? And is Marci seeing George because he is rich? Jimmy, this is just not like you." Jimmy, said nothing and went to bed at Tim's home for a change and not to sleep with Marci.

Tim watched at the meeting and Jimmy was flirting with this Venus. Marci was mad and flirted with George. Tim had no idea what kind of work they were doing for Larry. But Larry was pleased. Larry was also talking about seeing aliens from other worlds. Mr. King said Larry was on drugs like Joey had been and put Larry in rehab. Tim told no one but how was he going to run the company of Larry's without Larry? Tim went to Jimmy for help and said, "How am I going to run Larry's company while he is in rehab?"

Jimmy replied, "The same way you have always been running it all along. Larry was never here anyway, and you did all the work so what differences does it make? But I can stay with you awhile to help."

Tim asked, "What, you get time off for each killing or something?"

Jimmy answered, "I do not kill people. I am an agent and not a hitman. But, as in any job, I do get vacation and sick leave time. Do you want my help or not?" Tim nodded, yes.

After summer with the group, Jimmy came home each month for the meetings, then Halloween with the kids. Thanksgiving, Margo went with them to church to keep the guys out of trouble. Tim had made up with all the ladies, and now they all loved him. So church went okay.

Christmas came, and Jimmy did see Marci but did not stay overnight. Joey just winked and smiled singing, "We are into money." Jimmy said nothing. Tim watch Jimmy close at the meetings, and he was with Venus a lot. She wore diamonds and was pretty and very, very rich. Tim did Larry's company, and Jimmy was right, it was easy. Everyone just did what he told them to and never missed Larry. The money was coming in from the government contracts, and all was good. Another year passed with Marci not coming with Jimmy anywhere or to Sue's. Jimmy was back at work and who missed Jimmy the most, Tim, Margo, Marci, or Venus?

Then without calling, Jimmy came to Tim's house and laid on the couch. He said nothing and was very quiet. Tim came out saying, "Jimmy I did not know you were coming home." Then Tim sees blood all over Jimmy's shirt. Jimmy's shot and more than once. Tim ran to the phone and called Gerald to come fast. It looked like Jimmy had lost a lot of blood. Tim asked, "What happened? We should go to the hospital. I called Gerald." Gerald came in twenty minutes and started to work on Jimmy, removing the bullets. Tim just did what Gerald said.

Gerald said, "Now Jimmy, I am going to give you a shot to help with the pain, but it may make you a little silly so be careful." The medication was strong, and Jimmy started to talk silly. He called Marci first to find the guys who did this to him. She was to take George with her. Then he had Tim call Venus to come down and clean him up. Jimmy was not having the guys do it. Venus came into the house as Gerald was leaving. When Venus saw Jimmy all bloody, she cried.

Jimmy saw her pretty white ruffled shirt and said, "Take off the white shirt and wash me up, please. I do not want you to get blood on it." To Tim's surprise, Venus took off her top and started to wash Jimmy in her bra. Then Jimmy took off his t-shirt and Venus stopped. Jimmy said, "Never seen a guy without his shirt? Or too much hair on my chest for you?" Venus was still crying and shaking. Jimmy continued by saying, "Have you not touched a guy chests before?" Tim got more warm water and washed clothes.

Venus replied, "Okay, I have never been with a man, but I don't want to talk about my lack of a sex life." She continued to wash Jimmy's chest and helped him with a clean t-shirt.

Jimmy answered, "My private parts need washing too. I got blood there. Now don't look, wash me. And why have you not had sex? I am sure you have had a lot of opportunities. Not short of guys after you. You are very pretty and sexy."

Tim just had to say something, "Jimmy, stop teasing the girl and let her work on cleaning you. Are you sure you want her hands down there on you? The girl has a big crush on you. Maybe she is saving herself for you."

Jimmy just smiled and said, "Can I stay at your place tonight? Marci is out looking for the guys who did this to me. But this is the first place they will come to find me. I promise I will be good. I am in no mood for any action tonight."

Venus just nodded yes and helped Jimmy into her car. Tim followed Jimmy into Venus's car and to her place they went. When they got there, her house was a castle full of gold things. Venus's brother was waiting for her. Venus put Jimmy in her bed and Tim told Venus's brother all that had happened. Tim and her brother had wine, and Tim fell asleep.

It was morning, and Venus was standing over Tim. Her brother was making breakfast. Venus said, "Jimmy wants you." Venus appeared to be a little upset. Maybe Jimmy was sick. So Tim went to him.

Jimmy said, "Close the door. What did I do? Did I have sex with Venus last night? Ask her." Tim tried not to laugh, but it was funny. Jimmy just kept saying to himself, "What did I do?"

Tim answered, "I am not asking her that, let's get out of here." So, a fast goodbye, thanks a lot, and out the door. They went and took Venus's car home as she threw the keys to them.

Gerald was waiting for them and took one look at Jimmy then started to laugh. Gerald said, "See what all the washing got you. You got the girl all worked up. I hope you used protection." Jimmy looked even sicker and just went to his room, closed the door and went to sleep. He must have thought it was a bad dream. But it wasn't. Gerald told the whole town the news.

Sue came over, but Jimmy just stayed in bed for three days. Tim brought him food for those days and then Jimmy got up. Jimmy said, "I will talk to her about it. We are grownups."

Gerald was laughing, saying, "Oh, that will work. Talk to women. That always works after three days of not calling them. Having sex with women makes them crazier than they always are."

Jimmy replied, "Shut up Gerald and don't tell anyone." Tim wanted to tell Jimmy it was too late but said nothing. Sue came back and asked Jimmy to bring Venus to Thanksgiving. Jimmy agreed just to get Sue to go home without any more questions. Then Jimmy called Venus and asked her to come with him to Thanksgiving lunch with Sue and the family. Jimmy never talked about what happened that night. He was playing it cool. Tim thought that was a good idea for if she was pregnant, then he could marry her, if not, he could break it off with her. Jimmy did tell Venus he was very sick for three days and she was okay with that. They talked for a long time. Things appeared to be going good but how was Jimmy going to tell Marci? Jimmy got off the phone as Marci came through the door and Tim hid as Marci screamed at Jimmy. Bad words came out of Marci's mouth. She called Jimmy every name in the book, and he just sat there taking it, saying nothing. Then Marci left, and Jimmy was still alive but very quiet. Tim tried hard not to laugh, but it was funny.

Thanksgiving Day came, and the whole family watched to see Venus, Jimmy's new girlfriend. Joey was dancing around singing, "We're into money." Sue told him to shut up more than once. Jimmy's car came with Venus and him. Margo was mad; this was Jimmy's girlfriend he was going to marry? Venus had to go, in Margo's mind. Jimmy came in and helped Venus off with her coat. He never did that but for Margo. Jimmy introduced Venus to everyone, starting with Margo. She smiled but Margo was going to get her and good, she was toast.

Venus said, "My brother is coming too, I hope that is okay?" Sue smiled okay. Then Venus's brother came in a big car with a driver to the house. He came in, and Jimmy introduced him to everyone. Jimmy said the prayer and they started to eat. Venus said, "What different dishes you have, no two are the same. How nice."

Joey replied, "Only the best sale china for my family and friends." Everyone laughed but Venus and her brother, they were not eating.

Jimmy whispered to Venus, "Why are you not eating?"

Venus whispered back to Jimmy, but everyone was listening, "No one put food on our plates. Where are those people that do that for you?"

Jimmy replied, "We do that for ourselves. Just grab food and eat it. Be careful not to get too close to anyone's mouth." Venus and her brother did do that, but her brother almost got bit. Jimmy said, "They are our guests, let them have food."

After they were done eating, Venus asked, "Where are the people that clean up?"

Jimmy replied, "We like to do that ourselves too."

Joey could not help himself and cried, "No we don't. Where are those people?" Everyone was laughing, but Venus and her brother, they just smiled.

Then Venus asked, "Can I take Margo shopping for some new dresses for the holidays? I know the mall is open and I have some money." Sue and Joey just shook their head, yes and they were off in the big car her brother came in. Venus' brother watched TV with Joey and Tim, drinking beer. All appeared to be good until the phone call from the mall. Margo was calling Jimmy that she was lost and didn't know where Venus was. Margo was crying. Jimmy was out the door in a flash to the mall to find sweet little Margo. Tim and Sue followed and found Venus in a dressing room with no clothes. Margo had taken Venus' clothes as she tried on a dress for Jimmy that Margo told her he would love. Jimmy was all upset with Venus, and she was crying. Margo was smiling. Had Margo won and broke them up or was there more to come? Tim just sat back and watched. Talking to Jimmy was useless.

The holidays came, and Jimmy came alone to everything. He did stop at Marci's. Then on cold day in January, Venus' brother walked into Tim's office and said, "Where is Jimmy? Venus is pregnant, and he is the father." Tim didn't know what to say, he just sat there in silence.

After a minute or so, Tim got his breath and said, "Jimmy called Margo every night for prayers. I will tell him then. I will get back to you after I talk to Jimmy." Tim did see Gerald by the door, and now everyone knew and laughter was heard. As Venus' brother left and all the guys had a big smile on their faces, but now Tim had to tell Jimmy. Jimmy did want to be a father, right?

Tim went out to Sue's place to be with little Margo when Jimmy called. Joey had already told Sue the news. Joey was all smiles, singing his money song when Jimmy called Margo to do their prayers for the night. Then Margo said, "Uncle Tim is here and wants to talk to you. Everyone is very happy about something." Margo gave Tim the phone.

Tim said, "Venus' brother came to see me today, and she is pregnant. He says it is your baby and he wants to talk to you." It was very quiet for a long time.

Jimmy answered, "I will be home in the morning. Don't tell anyone." Before Tim could answer, Jimmy hung up the phone and maybe that was best. Tim put little Margo to bed and said Jimmy would explain in the morning. Then Tim sat with the family and talked about the money.

In the morning, Jimmy walked into Tim's house looking not happy. He repeated to himself, "What did I do?" Then he said, "Tim come with me to get an engagement ring and red roses for Venus. I will ask her to marry me." Tim just went with Jimmy, not saying a word. They went to the store with diamonds, and Jimmy, said, "How can I even pick out a ring when she has every kind of diamond? I don't even know what Venus likes. I don't know her, help!"

Tim went into action and said, "Well, we do know she loves you. We do know she has sex with you. So, if the ring is from you, she will love it. Now not too big a diamond so she can wear it all her life." Jimmy looked even sadder. Jimmy got a ring he liked and a dozen long-stemmed red roses on the way. Then he called Venus' brother for a meeting to talk. Everyone was calling Tim to know what was happening but Tim told them nothing, to wait and see.

Jimmy met with Venus' brother alone, and it must have gone well because Jimmy came back alive. Then Jimmy called Venus for a date. He cleaned up very nice, and he called little Margo to cancel for the first time their night prayer time on the phone but promised he would explain Sunday after church. After talking to Margo, Jimmy went to get Venus for their date. To Tim's surprise, Jimmy said, "Want to come with?" Tim nodded yes, and they left.

Jimmy took Tim to Venus' home and left him there with her brother who was very nice. They drank wine and laughed until Jimmy returned with Venus. Venus was all happy, and they were engaged to be married. Venus asked Jimmy to stay the night, and he looked at her brother, but he just smiled it was okay. Jimmy went to bed with Venus and Tim slept in the living room. Jimmy could not sleep, and he woke Tim at 3 AM to go. With goodbyes to Venus and her brother, they left. But Jimmy did not drive home, he went straight to Marci's. Jimmy talked to Marci in a low voice. Tim could not hear a word. But then Jimmy and Marci went to bed. Tim slept on his bed chair thing in the same room. Jimmy slept until 10 AM; they left just in time for church. Tim said to Jimmy, "I think you better make up your mind between these two women." When they got to church Jimmy saw Margo right away, and she ran up to him. He just took her hand, and they sat down as church was starting. They sat with Sue and the boys.

After church, on the way out, Jimmy asked Margo, "How old are you now?" Margo giggled and hugged Jimmy.

Margo replied, "I am eight years old, and I will be wearing the pretty white dress for church."

Jimmy answered, "I know you are not a little girl anymore. I can't carry you around anymore like a little girl or sit on my lap. We will have to get you that pretty white dress this week. You are old enough to say your prayers at night without me, now. I may not be able to call you each day. After lunch, we need to talk about something I did, and I am not okay with it." No more was said, and the boys were acting up with Sue trying to stop them. Jimmy looked at Tim very sad.

After lunch at which Joey was overly nice to Jimmy, Jimmy said, "Margo, we have to talk." Margo acted so grown up as she sat on a chair looking at Jimmy. Jimmy looked down and sadly said, "Venus and I are getting married. We are going to have a baby. I know you don't like her but give her another chance." Tim got a chair and sat down to listen with the family.

Margo started screaming and crying in the worst way. Jimmy looked for help, but no one spoke up.

Margo cried, "How did this happen? Did you have sex with her? Why?"

Now Tim spoke up and said, "Remember Jimmy, we always tell Margo the truth. She is our little angel. Please continue." Jimmy's face was all red, and he just looked down.

Jimmy said, "We talked about where babies come from in science homework. Yes, I did have sex with her, and I am sorry if I upset you by this." Then Jimmy just got up and left the house. Jimmy was crying in the car all the way to Tim's house, and Tim could hardly stop laughing.

Margo cried and called Marci. Marci was as unhappy about Jimmy marrying Venus, having that baby as Margo was and the plan was on to get rid of Venus somehow. Jimmy stopped crying and said, "I have to make this up to Margo and Marci somehow. What do you think, Tim?"

Tim did not want to answer, but he did. "Jimmy, I can check to see if Venus' baby is yours. You need to stop sleeping with Marci before Venus finds out. Take Margo on a special trip for her church thing. Maybe Disney World, that may help Margo."

Jimmy replied, "Okay, Disney World for Margo may help. I am still going to work with Marci, and nothing can change that. Yes, I want to be a father, but I am not sure of Venus."

Tim asked, "How are you going to keep the two women apart? I mean not killing each other. What is the plan?"

Larry was at Tim's door saying, "Mr. King and my mom want to give Jimmy and Venus an engagement party. When would you like it? It would be in their home. What do you say, Jimmy? Stop the gossip." Tim just shook his head.

Jimmy replied, "I will have to ask Venus about it and get back to you."

Larry laughed and said, "Yes, Jimmy, your life is over. But you got one thing right, always ask the women first. Women will tell you everything, so thinking is no longer needed for you to do for yourself. Be a good husband and take your orders from her." Then Tim walked Larry to the door before Jimmy would hit him because Jimmy wanted to hit something.

As the months followed, Jimmy and Tim took Margo and the boys to Disney World. Margo loved it, and she with Marci had a plan to get that Venus out of Jimmy's life but how? Jimmy talked with Charles about starting a university for students who wanted to work for Larry, and this would bring in a lot of money. The guys would each teach one class on what they did for Larry's company. Jimmy would teach music, science, math, and sex education. But when he worked as a spy, Tim would cover his classes. Jimmy planned to stop being a spy and be home every night with his wife and child as a teacher. Jimmy bought a house next to Tim's and had a bedroom for Venus' brother to stay over whenever he wanted. There was also a bedroom for Margo. Time went by with birthdays and Easter, but Jimmy still slept with Marci at night. Tim said nothing and helped cover it up so Venus would not find out.

Then came Jimmy and Venus' engagement party at Mr. King's house. Jimmy got Margo a very pretty new dress with rainbow colors and princess shoes. Venus had a purple dress that changed color when she moved, very nice. But Venus was not feeling the best, and she did show that she was pregnant. The party looked like a war zone, Jimmy's Marci and her people on one side and Venus' with her friends on the other side of the room. It was like the war families of the Hatfield and the McCoy in history. They would not mix or have a good time. The food was great, no gifts, but dancing music and Jimmy danced with Margo all night. Venus looked happy but pale. Then after the party, Jimmy and Venus went to his place where he had the housekeeper and her husband to help Venus rest. Venus got sick, and Jimmy went for his housekeeper to watch Venus as he went to get Tim. It was like a flash and Tim was there, but it was too late. Venus started having the baby a few months too soon, and there was no stopping it. The baby was born dead, and it was a boy. Jimmy sat holding his son and cried. Tim worked to help Venus, and she would be okay. Jimmy named the baby James John Elgin. They checked to see why the baby died but there was little to understand on this. Jimmy had to tell Venus, and he did go into the bedroom.

All he heard was Venus screaming, "No." Gerald came to recheck everything and Jimmy had a small funeral for his son, James. A small grave at the top of a hill between Jimmy and Tim's houses. The local pastor said a few words. Venus was too upset to come. Everyone knew because Gerald told everyone. Margo and Marci went out for milkshakes, and they were pleased because they didn't want Jimmy and Venus to marry.

Time went by, and Jimmy stayed with Venus at her home unless he was spying at work. But Jimmy still was sleeping with Marci. There was no Venus for Halloween, Thanksgiving, or Christmas; Jimmy just came alone. But Valentines Day Jimmy took Venus out to eat and said, "We can have other children. Just give yourself time to heal." On Jimmy's birthday in February he was with Margo and Tim, just like old times together.

Charles' wife, Penny, had a big party planned for his birthday, and Charles was Jimmy's partner at the university, so Jimmy and Venus were to come. Jimmy had told Venus he would meet her there because Margo's birthday was in a few days and Margo wanted red shoes that night. Jimmy knew Margo's shoe size but what color red did she want? Jimmy bought a few pairs of shoes and drove out to Sue's before Charles' party. Jimmy got there, and Margo was waiting.

Margo said, "I can be your girlfriend now. I am all grown up. You do not need Venus anymore." Jimmy looked confused and just nodded then left. But Margo hid in the back seat of his car. As Jimmy drove to Charles' home, Margo sat up and kissed Jimmy's neck; she had on red lipstick. Jimmy was so surprised he turned and drove right into a tree. Jr. Joey was driving in his dad's pick up without a license again and stopped to help. Jimmy was just worried about Margo. Jr. Joey promised to take Margo home, and they would talk about it later. Margo was crying because she was afraid Jimmy was mad at her. Margo was not hurt. Jr. Joey dropped Jimmy off at Charles' birthday party so he could get a ride home with Venus. Jr. Joey and Margo waited for no one to see Jr. Joey was driving without a license.

Jimmy walked through the door, and Penny took his coat. Venus saw the red lipstick on his neck and went crazy. She started throwing food at Jimmy. First Charles' birthday cake then any food she could grab. The guys were hiding behind the living room furniture and jumping up to get the flying food. It looked very silly, and Tim grabbed Jimmy down saying, "Run for it man, women are crazy." Jimmy got up and tried to talk to Venus, but she, slapped him across the face, then put her engagement ring in his hand and left. Jr. Joey and Margo saw it all from the window, they hid as she came out. Jimmy was behind her, but he just went to Tim's house. Tim took Jimmy home. The guys were laughing so hard and eating off the floor.

The next day it was the talk of the town. Everyone was laughing, and Jimmy was very upset. Jimmy asked, "Why did she do that? I think I have been a dump." Tim did not know what to say, so he took Jimmy out for a root beer float and Jimmy agreed that did make him feel better.

After a few days, Jimmy came out of his bedroom saying, "I think I want to go away to school to study to be a doctor like you, Tim." Tim was sure he just wanted to find out why his son died. Tim found a university in Minnesota and Jimmy left that Monday. Jimmy did tell Tim he would write Venus as soon as some time had passed.

Tim had a question to ask, "Why did you not come with Venus to Charles' party? The two of you could have taken those shoes to Margo." Jimmy's answer floored Tim.

Jimmy said, "Charles and Penny's kids always call me grandpa because of my relationship with Charles' mother. I have not told Venus about it, and I am not going to. Can you understand that? I will write to her about it and see where things go from there."

After Jimmy was gone a few weeks, Tim asked Venus, "Why did you throw food at Jimmy?"

Venus said, "Because he had red lipstick on his neck. Jimmy has not touched me since the baby died." Tim did not know what to say, so he just nodded and left. Did she know about Marci?

Jimmy did call Tim, Margo, and Marci each weekend. Tim remembered how hard medical school was. Tim did not know Jimmy's plans to work as a spy while teaching at the university or what? Tim did teach Jimmy's classes but was not very good at it. Jimmy helped by phone and sent videos for the students to watch. Jimmy also did those lesson plans for Tim.

Jimmy did not come home for Halloween; he said Margo was older now and should go with her girlfriends. But Margo loved going with Tim and Jimmy. She missed them. Jimmy did come home for Thanksgiving and Christmas, but he was very tired. They did have fun, Tim and Jimmy, but Jimmy still went to sleep at Marci's place. Joey tried to get Jimmy and Venus back together, but Jimmy said, "She dumped me, and I want to stay dumped." That was the end of it with Venus.

For Jimmy's birthday, Margo and Tim decided to drive down and surprise Jimmy. When they got there, it was like a big city hospital. Tim found the place Jimmy was staying, and the guy at the desk told them what room Jimmy was staying in. Margo and Tim knocked on the door. A woman answered, "Come in." So they did as Jimmy came out of the bathroom with no shirt on. The blonde-haired woman stayed in the shadows of the room. Tim put his hands over Margo's eyes.

Margo said, "Stop it, I want to see." Jimmy had his shirt on by that time, and the woman was out of sight.

Jimmy asked, "Why did you not call first? Go to the café, and I will meet you there in a few minutes." Tim and Margo went to the place Jimmy said, and Jimmy showed up about five minutes later alone. They did not talk about the woman in Jimmy's room, and each time Margo tried to talk about it, Tim changed the subject. They stayed that night at Jimmy's room for his birthday and then drove back with a promise from Tim to Jimmy that he would always call first before they came. Jimmy was home for Margo's birthday but not the summer. Tim and Margo did miss Jimmy, but he gave them his phone number there so they could call anytime. Margo called a lot and never did a woman answer. Jimmy came home again for Thanksgiving, Christmas and their birthdays. Other than that, it was just phone calls and letters until Jimmy graduated from Medical school. Jimmy didn't go to his graduation; he just took the paper sooner to be home with Tim and Margo. He went over.

Jimmy walked through Tim's door that spring day and just laid on the couch. The guys said Jimmy had too many girls after him and he was all tired out. But Tim knew Jimmy was a one-woman kind of guy. Jimmy was not sleeping with Marci anymore. What was going on? Then Margo called Tim crying, "Marci called and said she is getting married. She wants me to be her bridesmaid. Is Jimmy marrying Marci?" Tim did not know what to say but would ask Jimmy who was asleep now. When Jimmy awoke, Tim told him to call Margo. Tim had not a clue what was going on, but Jimmy asked Sue if he could talk to Margo about something special.

Margo said, "Is Marci getting married? She told me she was. She wants me to be her bridesmaid. Are you marrying Marci?" Jimmy put his arm around Margo, Tim hid for safety.

Jimmy said, "Yes, Marci is getting married this summer. You would make a great bridesmaid. You could help her with her wedding. But I am not marrying Marci. She is marrying George, her partner from our group. I am giving the bride away. Please be at the wedding as my date." Margo was all smiles, and the wedding didn't happen that summer because of all the planning.

The holidays passed and on Valentines Day, Marci and George had a beautiful wedding with red and white. Margo had the best time, and all was good. Margo had another problem, she wanted a training bra, and Sue was too busy to take her. Margo called Uncle Tim, who was not listening to her and said, "Jimmy will take you shopping." So Margo called him.

Jimmy picked up Margo at home to take shopping, but he didn't know what Margo needed. Sue had not even listened to Margo either. When they got to the mall, Jimmy asked, "What are we shopping for, a new dress, toys, or stuffed animals?"

Margo replied, "I need a training bra. Uncle Tim said you could take me. Mom is too busy with the baby." Jimmy just sat there thinking. My guess would be he was thinking of killing Tim or Sue. Maybe he thought they need to be trained first, so it is called a training bra?

Jimmy then said, "Okay, I can do this. It is just clothing girls need. Okay, Margo, let's go to the women's area, and the lady clerks will help us." They went to the lady's wear, and Jimmy told the sales clerk what they needed. Margo was to pick out about a dozen in all colors but a few in white. Margo noticed the sale ladies did flirt with Jimmy, he was nice but didn't flirt back. Then home they went after ice cream and Jimmy talked with Sue in a very low voice.

Margo didn't want Jimmy to get into trouble, so she said, "Jimmy knows a lot about bras, and he was a big help to me with the sale ladies."

Joey laughed and said, "I bet Jimmy does, but from now on your mother will be taking you shopping." Not another word about it, and Jimmy was very nice about it but from that date on, Sue took Margo shopping for everything. Margo was happy because Jimmy was home and she would flirt with him as the sales ladies did in that store. But this time Jimmy would flirt back with Margo, and that was fun. Uncle Tim would laugh at them.

Jimmy also helped Margo with modeling classes. Margo wanted to be a movie star, so Jimmy and Tim bought shares in a movie company. Margo modeled teen clothes and did some acting, so she now had a little money of her own. Margo wanted to live with Tim, but her parents were not okay with that because Jimmy lived there most of the time when he was not working as an agent. Tim worried a lot about Jimmy when he was on an assignment. Tim told Sue and Joey, "Jimmy has a girlfriend, and I think it is serious. I have not met her. I don't think she is good for Jimmy. When Jimmy sees her, he is very happy, but if he doesn't, he is sad."

Sue was concerned, but Tim was afraid if they said anything to Jimmy about his new girlfriend he may leave and never come back to them. Margo was just pleased to have

Jimmy around a lot more. Tim had a lot of people coming to see him in his office and Jimmy would take Margo to lunch or the movies. Tim even made a deal with Jimmy he could bring his new girlfriend to the house to sleep in his bedroom. Tim would not even come out to see her, they'd have complete privacy. The boys did try to see her, and she was pretty, blonde with brown eyes. Merit said, "She bounces all over when she walks."

Mark said, "She always wore black clothes and drove a black sports car." Tim was going to keep his promise and not look at her because he was sure Jimmy would notice. How Jimmy knew things, people thought Tim was not sure, but if Jimmy were an alien from another world, Tim would not say a word about it. Was that because Jimmy was his best friend or because when Larry did, they put him in rehab. Tim did not want to stop drinking liquor. He needed it.

Tim had a wife and daughter in Paris, France with his in-laws, a daughter with his boss's wife who he was still sleeping with, a son, Merit to raise at home and don't even start on his brother's wife with kids. Tim did not think he liked his brother, Joey but he knew he did like his best friend, Jimmy. People in the town and employees came to Tim for help with problems. Tim did what he could to solve them, and mostly money worked. Tim knew Larry would want to help them, so he just took more of Larry's money to help. One day Sue came in to find Margo, and a townsperson came to see Tim, he called him Godfather. Was this like that movie or was it a faith thing? Sue was questioning it. Tim did not answer her and Jimmy just said, "Margo, please go with your mother now." Margo did go with Sue, but Sue never forgot it, and she never got a straight answer about it from Tim or Jimmy. What was going on there?

Margo said to Tim, "I want to come and live with you. I am afraid at home." When Jimmy heard this, he was all for Margo coming to live with Tim.

Jimmy said, "I will move out to live in my home where my housekeeper is. Or I can live in the house Venus and I were going to have together. I also have the home with Marci. I can go anywhere, but Margo needs you."

Tim replied, "I think Joey is just too strict for Margo and she wants to date boys now. Margo thinks she could get us to let her do anything as she always has. I see through her pretty face." But Tim did talk to Sue about it, and Margo got her way again. Tim reminded Sue that Jimmy had a girlfriend and this would be an issue for Margo if she lived with him when Jimmy came with her. Sue was okay with it then, and Jimmy stopped coming with his girlfriend at night. Jimmy did stay at one of his other homes, an unused house next to Tim, Jimmy will enlarge Tim's home. Tim and Jimmy tore down Jimmy's home that he and Venus were going to live in and he just took all the stuff out to Tim's house. The basement had a machine in it.

Margo asked, "What kind of machine is this?" The boys could see Tim didn't want to answer, but he did and told the truth.

Tim said, "It was going to be a time machine, believe it or not? I wanted to know what happened to my mother and sister, Jimmy wanted to find Sylvia, and Venus wanted to know about her parents because she never knew them. Venus' brother raised her. Venus had all the money we needed to get the supplies. I could get the supplies through Larry's company with no questions asked. Jimmy was the brain, and he did make the machine work, but it was for only a few seconds. Jimmy was alone that night, this was before Venus, and Jimmy's baby died. The machine had never worked again since then. I don't think Jimmy could have done much in a few seconds. We were looking at the past and trying to change something maybe or learn from seeing what did happen to all those people we loved." Margo was concerned but in a few seconds what could have possibly happened? So, she just watched to see if they ever got that machine to work again and they did work on it. Venus did want to give them the money, but Jimmy would not take it, and no more work moved ahead to find out more about Sylvia.

Tim was on the phone a lot with his wife, Betty. Tim called it phone sex. Jimmy would say, "Tim, please close the door. You are making me sick. I don't want to hear this."

Things were going pretty good. Margo was living with Tim, and her parents wanted her to date boys her age. The first date was Bobby Jameson, Jim's son, the guy that was there during Jimmy's first job cleaning out his horse barns. Jimmy sat there cleaning his gun as Bobby came to pick Margo up for their date. Tim said to the frightened Bobby, "Did you know we have many family members that are crazy. I wonder if it is inherited?" Margo just gave Tim a look like stop it.

Jimmy said, "I will be cleaning my gun all night, so I will be still up when you bring Margo home and not too late, I hope." Bobby just nodded and ran for the door. Margo followed him but from that time on all Margo's dates went pretty much the same way. No one was going to touch Margo with her two uncles around, and they were always around when date night came. Then to make things worse, Tim had Merit and Mark follow Margo on her date each time.

Margo had just about enough of this, and she went to talk to Uncle Tim. Margo said, "I will die a virgin. Could you please let one of my dates at least kiss me goodnight?"

Tim gave Margo an answer she couldn't forget. Tim said, "Jimmy would be very displeased with you if you had sex with any of these boys before you are married. Even kissing may be a problem for him. A kiss on the hand, okay. It is against Jimmy's church beliefs. So you will have to be a good girl until you are twenty-one or Jimmy will have to kill them. Then Jimmy would go to jail, and you don't want that do you?" Margo agreed with Tim. Joey and Sue were very pleased to know that all the boys were afraid to do anything with their little angel Margo or her uncle would hurt them bad. All boys knew Margo was off limits to just holding hands.

CHAPTER THREE

JIMMY ELGIN, IT HURTS SO MUCH, BUT I LOVE HER!

Jimmy and Tim continued to move the stuff out of Jimmy's house as it was torn down. Margo had a new bedroom and bathroom in Tim's house. There were more bathrooms and another shower in the basement. One could never have too many bathrooms. Jimmy made a basement cave-like for just the time machine and some things of his own. Was he going to stay there? Then Tim saw papers on children that Marci and Jimmy had in their care. Jimmy could not sleep without his woman, and he never came with her to Tim's house after Margo moved in, so what was up there? Jimmy worked a lot in the basement at night, so one night Tim went down to ask some question. Tim said, "Where do you want these papers of the children you and Marci have?"

Jimmy laughed and answered, "None of these children are mine and Marci's. They have parents but are very poor, and we help them out. The home I have there is for Marci and George too, who stays there sometimes. Marci is going to have a baby."

Tim replied, "Is the baby yours? Should I check to see the bloodwork? How many children live in that big house of yours?"

Jimmy answered with a smile, "The baby is George's, Marci's husband. I do not need you to check for me. I know it is not mine. There are about three thousand children, but not all live in my old house. I help with things like food and clothes, toys for Christmas and Easter stuff."

Tim helped Jimmy get food from a food bank for the kids and on Halloween, Jimmy needed truckloads of pumpkins to carve which they ate the insides on Thanksgiving. For Christmas, Jimmy needed a Santa Claus and it could not be him. So Tim got a Santa's suit to wear for those children. Margo now had dances at Halloween with Tim and Jimmy volunteering to be the chaperons. They even sang songs for the kids to dance to. Tim danced with all the girls and women, but Jimmy only danced with Margo. Even when the women teachers came to ask him, he would go up and sing a song until these women went away. Jimmy sang most of the night. He was very nice to the women teachers, and these women did flirt with Jimmy, but he did not flirt back. He was on the phone a lot to his girlfriend, Tim guessed.

When Jimmy was not with his girlfriend for a while, he was very moody and hard to get along with. Tim could hear Jimmy talking to his girlfriend, and he wanted to see her more and more. Margo was busy with school and her friends now, so she did not notice. Jimmy was always nice to her and Margo did have a big crush on Jimmy, as did all of Margo's girlfriends. Jimmy was the cool spy or secret agent man.

Sue wanted Jimmy to bring his new girlfriend to Thanksgiving lunch. Tim said, "You have to ask Jimmy. But don't upset him. Jimmy is very touchy about this new girlfriend of his."

Sue started, "Jimmy, the pipe in the basement is dripping. Can you and Tim check it on Thanksgiving? Could you also bring your new girlfriend? We want to meet her."

Jimmy looked at Tim and then said, "We can check the pipe in the basement after church. Can Margo come with us to church?" Sue nodded yes. Then Jimmy continued "No, she is not coming with me. Maybe next year. She is cooking for your parents and sister's family."

Tim said, "We were not that bad to those other women you came with to Thanksgiving. Okay, we should not have said anything about Marci eating with her fingers or throwing food. But with Venus, that was all Margo. Please give us another chance. Are you going to her family to eat?"

Jimmy just shook his head no and walked away. Tim could see Jimmy was very moody again. Sue handed the list of things to get at the grocery store for her to make Thanksgiving meal with all their favorites. Margo went with to help the guys find everything so they knew what to get.

In a few days, it was the morning of Thanksgiving, and they went to church with Margo then to Sue's place. They set out to check the pipe in the basement that was dripping, but Jimmy noticed right away there was a woman in the boys' bedroom. Tim was talking to Sue and Margo was changing out of her church dress. Jimmy called, "Tim get down here, now!"

Tim came down the stairs asking. "Is the pipe dripping that bad?" Jimmy just pointed to the woman in the bed with little clothes on. Tim looked and then he looked again. Tim sat down a minute. His eyes growing big. Margo came down the stair. Tim asked, "Who is that woman in Jr. Joey's bed? She has very few clothes on!"

Jimmy looked at Tim like he was crazy and said, "Nothing gets by you does it, Tim? She is in your nephew's bed who is how old? And don't even think of asking me what she is doing there. I think we both know. I am calling the police. Jr. Joey is just a kid, and she is how old?"

Margo added by saying, "That is Jr. Joey's girlfriend. He found her on the streets. She was homeless. Don't tell mom or dad because they will not understand, okay? Her name is Jenny. She is older than Jr. Joey but not that much. Mark sleeps out here, and Merit does when he comes. Jr. Joey makes them hanging things to sleep on."

Jimmy went for the phone, but Tim stopped him by saying, "Let's talk this over with Jr. Joey and his parents before we do anything." Jr. Joey had just walked down the stair with Mark and Merit. Tim continued, "Jr. Joey, let's bring your girlfriend upstairs for your parents to meet. How long has this been going on? Where is your family? Is she a runaway? Who is she?" Then Jenny showed Tim her drivers license. They started upstairs. Mark and Merit went first.

Jimmy said, "What do we do, take her upstairs and start eating after prayer? Do you think they will notice?"

Tim replied, "Yes, that is the plan. We'll all sit down, start eating after prayer and wait for Joey or Sue to notice then, Jr. Joey, you have to tell them. Jr. Joey looked afraid and took his girlfriend up to eat. Jimmy sat there waiting to see how long it would take Joey or Sue to notice.

Joey said, "Jimmy are you not going to say the prayer?" Jimmy said the prayer and waited.

Sue asked, "What about the pipe in the basement? Do we need to call a plumber? Did you guys even look at it?"

Tim answered, "No, I can't say we did. We did not even look at it, sorry. Something else got our attention. Please pass the peas." Sue just stopped eating and looked at Tim then Jimmy. Sue saw Jenny, and so did Joey, sitting by Jr. Joey.

Joey said, "Margo, you know you are to tell us first before you bring your girlfriends to Thanksgiving lunch. We need to save a place at the table for Jimmy's girlfriends." Jimmy just smiled. Tim was filling his plate, so was Merit and Mark. Jimmy started doing the same with a hold for his and Margo's plates if they had to run for it.

Jr. Joey spoke up, "This is my girlfriend, and she has been living in the basement with me. That is what distracted Uncle Tim and Jimmy. I want to keep her." Jimmy slowly got up with his and Margo's plates, and they went into the living room to eat. Merit and Mark followed them with their plates of food. Tim stayed to face the music with Jr. Joey and his live-in girlfriend. What was said should never be repeated. The language was so bad Jimmy took the kids outside to eat, but it was cold. Then Jimmy took the kids to the movies and told them they would get pie later if things settled down at home. But it never did that night.

Merit cried, "What about my Dad? We better go back for him." Jimmy just shook his head, no. That night the kids stayed with Jimmy at Tim's place. Tim did come home with pie for all but not a word about what happened. In the weeks that passed, Jr. Joey was still alive, and his girlfriend still lived with them on an agreement to behavior which Sue required. Jenny helped Sue with the sick baby girl named Sally and Joey bragged about his son with a woman. Jimmy could not see it. Tim was more understanding of the rules.

The plumber was called and told everyone about Jr. Joey's live-in girlfriend, so the whole town knew. No one at school asked Jr. Joey about it. Were they too afraid of his uncles that would hurt them?

At Christmas, Sue walked into that church with her head held high and so did the whole family. Jr. Joey had his girlfriend's hand and they all sat in the front row. As you could guess, they were the talk of the town, but Jimmy was okay with that, at least no one was talking about his love life. Tim made sure Joey put extra money in the collection box as Jimmy always did. The pastor talked about not judging your neighbor and that we are all family. Sue was happy, and the question was, did Tim get to the pastor or was it Jimmy who talked to him to be nice?

Things got back to normal. Jr. Joey got a job with Larry at the company, and Margo still got to help Tim in the office with Jimmy. Margo was a cheerleader at school which Tim and Jimmy went to all the games that she cheered. Tim nor Jimmy had ever done sports because Jimmy worked after school and Tim was too sick. Merit nor Mark was in any sports, but they too came to all the games Margo cheered for at school.

Jr. Joey was graduating from high school that spring and then to college he would have to go if he was working for Larry. Larry would pay for his college and a paycheck as he did with Tim and Joey. It was a good deal and Jr. Joey loved working for Larry. At Jr. Joey's high school graduation, Jimmy did not come. Sue was very upset, and she asked Tim to talk to Jimmy. Tim said, "Why did you not come to Jr. Joey's graduation; Sue was very upset you didn't come."

Jimmy replied, "I couldn't go because Charles had a son graduating too and his mother would be there. I don't want to see her again, okay?" Tim understood and told Sue the truth about why Jimmy didn't come. Sue was not happy with Jimmy the way it was because he got Margo a new red sports car for her birthday. Jimmy had been teaching Margo to drive it. Joey was not happy about it, but Jimmy did pay for the insurance and gas.

Margo must have heard someone talking about Jimmy's new girlfriend being pregnant. Margo got so mad she drove the car as fast as she could away from home and off the road the car flipped. The police called Tim. Tim and Jimmy were at the accident within minutes. Margo was okay, but Jimmy carried her out of the car. Margo slapped Jimmy's face. Tim was not clear on why. Jimmy just turned his face, and he knew. Gerald checked Margo over at the hospital. Tim paid off the police, then asked Merit and Mark why Margo hit Jimmy. Merit said, "Because Jimmy's girlfriend is pregnant." Tim waited for Jimmy to tell him how many days.

Then one night, Jimmy came to Tim's bedroom door and knocked, "Tim, I have to tell you something. I am going to be a father. I am very happy about this, but I need to talk to Margo about it. What can I do or say to make this better for her?"

Tim replied, "I got this one for you. Congrats, you always wanted to be a father. When are you to marry? Would I like to meet the bride now? I am coming to your wedding, right?"

Jimmy answered slowly, "We are not getting married because she is already married. Her husband can't have children. But he doesn't know that. I was the doctor in Minnesota then."

Tim sat up in bed and said, "Are you sure it is yours? How nice of you to give your service in that way. I will tell Margo the truth." Jimmy just walked away and said no more about it. Tim explained it to Margo and told her that it would not last and Jimmy would leave this woman. Jimmy and his girlfriend did appear to be talking on the phone a lot with disagreements. But Thanksgiving was here again, and they got the food on Sue's list. Tim, Margo, and Jimmy did go to church the morning of Thanksgiving, praying a lot.

To Sue's they went and Joey asked the question Jimmy didn't want to answer. After prayer, Joey said, "What are the sins of the family this year? What do I not know?" No one talked, they just looked at one another and ate faster. Joey said, "No one needs to run with your plates."

Jimmy replied, "I am going to be a father. I am not getting married because she is already married. Her husband is sick and can't have children. I did the study on him myself."

Joey looked up and said, "It sounds like you did a little bit more than study the situation, Jimmy. I will make a deal with you. If you stop seeing this married woman with the sick husband, then I will go to church every Sunday with the family." Tim knew Joey was trying to help Jimmy and did care because Joey only went to church on Christmas. Jimmy just shook his head, no. Margo got up and left the table. Then Jimmy went home, and Tim followed him. After that, Tim did not see Jimmy for weeks. Marci called to remind Tim that he was to be Santa for the children at that place. The gifts for the children were there, but not Jimmy, so Tim had Merit and Mark help.

Then Jimmy's housekeeper called Tim to help Jimmy. Jimmy was laying on the floor crying. Tim asked, "What happened? Are you hurt? Who did this to you?"

Jimmy could hardly talk and said, "She and my baby are dead. It was a son; I named Travis Tim. When I got back, the doctors had moved her body, but I had to take my son." Jimmy had a grave for this son by the other boy, James who had died from Venus. Tim did not know what to say. He stayed with Jimmy and then they went to church for Christmas. Tim had told the family. As before, they all walked into the church with their head held high. Margo and Tim helped Jimmy. Jimmy had told Gerald, so all the town knew Jimmy's married girlfriend died in childbirth with his son. The pastor was very nice to Jimmy, and they all prayed for God's love.

Jimmy had to take time off from work as a secret agent. He was too upset to think. Gerald and Tim were the doctors who signed the papers for Jimmy's sick leave. Jimmy did not go anywhere; he stayed in bed crying and reading the bible. Tim stayed with Jimmy most of the time and just sent the guys notes on what to do. Larry was home and very nice to Jimmy. The whole town cried for Jimmy; this was two dead sons and two dead girlfriends. Merit and Mark made up a little song which Tim did not like, but it was something like "Another hits the dust, and another hits the dust." It did have a catching tone, but Jimmy would not have found it funny.

Tim told Merit, "If I hear you boys sing that song I will send you to live with your mother in Paris, France. Do you boys understand me? Merit and Mark, I could do that to you too." So the boys only sang it when Tim was nowhere in sight, but the guys did find it funny at work.

Jimmy went out for only a few minutes on New Years for the dance at Margo's school, but he did not sing anything and just watched. Tim stayed close to Jimmy. Margo did not want to stay at the dance that New Year's Eve but Tim told her to or Jimmy would be sad if she left.

For Valentine, Jimmy got Margo something but stayed home at Tim's house. Tim stayed with him. Tim asked, "Do you know why she died in childbirth? Was there something I could have done to help save the baby or her?" Margo came over with a nice card for Jimmy and overheard them talking. Margo wanted to hear Jimmy answer Tim's question on those deaths.

Jimmy replied, "The baby came too soon, only five months and he did not have much of a chance. But I think they would have just thrown him away as they do with abortions. Her husband would not have paid the cost of a funeral for my son but her, I don't know where they took her. And please don't say it, another one to find. I am never going to marry, am I?"

Tim smiled and said, "You will find someone to marry. You are young, and women your age are looking for a good husband and father. And you can make good money to support a family. You are handsome, good looking, smart, and just a nice guy. A little moody sometimes."

Margo came in with her card saying, "I will marry you anytime you want. I can give you children. I will not die in childbirth; I am healthy and young."

Jimmy, smiled and answered, "If you still want me when you are twenty-one than that is a deal."

Gerald came in saying, "Jimmy, I got two daughters. You can have both. You can even have my wife. Please take them." Everyone was laughing as Jimmy just shook his head no thanks.

Jimmy continued but was having a very hard time. For his birthday, Margo and Tim decided to take him somewhere special, to Spain on the beach. That is where they met Steve, a very rich boy and Tim with Jimmy liked him. Steve was after Margo, and he was sure to check with Tim and Jimmy before he did anything to their sweet little Margo. Steve and his parents took Margo out to see Spain and Tim with Jimmy just stayed in their room to rest. Margo was not sure she should go, but it appeared to please Jimmy, so she did. Margo knew she did not love Steve, but he was a very nice guy and could give her anything she wanted. She would date him until she was older and could marry Jimmy at twenty-one. Not long to wait for love.

They got back from Spain and Margo continued to date Steve. On her birthday, he had a surprise party at his mansion home for her. All of Margo's friends were impressed. Jimmy gave Margo a silver necklace with a heart that ticked, but he did not stay long. Steve took Margo to her school prom and then her graduation from High School. Jimmy came to both but didn't stay long. Margo wrote Tim a letter about how much she loved Jimmy, romantically. Tim wrote back after a few weeks saying, if love is real, true, and right, it will wait until you are twenty-one. Give Jimmy's heart time to heal. So Margo went off to college with Mark and Merit with Steve.

Margo and the boys came home more just for weekends, holiday, and birthdays. Mrs. King, Larry's mom died right before Margo's birthday, she was coming home anyway. Margo did not live with Steve or even kiss him on the mouth, but he was okay with that. They were waiting to marry because of Jimmy's faith in his church. Steve understood, and they were best friends, him and Jimmy.

Margo was going to college to be a doctor, and so was Merit. Mark was into research. Steve's education was about business to run his father's companies. Tim had asked the kids to come to Mrs. King's funeral. Larry was a mess over his mother's death. Mr. King was even worse over it. Tim had his hands full with the two of them. Steve couldn't come because of an issue at his dad's company. Merit and Mark came to help Tim with Larry and Mr. King. Margo went over to Jimmy and said, "I have missed you. What should we do for your birthday? I want to come home for it, maybe the three of us can do something, Tim, you, and me."

Jimmy replied, "Yes, we could go out to eat, the three of us. I am sorry I have been out of it for some time. Thanks for all the nice cards. I did send cards back. I did not know what to write; I didn't write anything in them. I hope the gifts were okay. Tim told me you were doing okay. How is Steve? I know he is busy taking over his father's busy companies."

Margo replied, "You liked Steve. You never come by to clean your gun as you did with my other dates and Tim never told him our family is crazy. I miss those days. I wish we could talk on the phone again. You could come down to college and see me, or I could come to see you. Remember when I was sweet sixteen and you sang all those songs to me on my birthday? I kissed you when you turned your face, and I got your check. Then on my eighteen birthday, you kissed me on my lips and dad got so mad." Margo moved very close to Jimmy, flirting.

Jimmy did not move away, he just replied, "You're going to be twenty-one at your next birthday, right?" Margo smiled, nodded yes and took Jimmy's hand, walking out to the grave site to lose Merit and Mark. After Margo went back to school for a few weeks, Jimmy went for a lot of long walks. Tim was worried but what could he do? Tim was so busy with Larry and Mr. King.

Then Mr. King died. Margo and the boys came home for that funeral too. Margo had not dressed well, the weather had been warm but then turned very cold, so Jimmy gave her his coat. Margo was so pleased to be so close to Jimmy, but Jimmy got a bad cold. Margo called Tim, but he was so busy with Larry. What would Larry do without his stepfather and his money?

At Margo's birthday party, Steve got down on one knee and asked her to marry him. Jimmy did not stay, he just went home early. He left a small gift with a silver ring in it. Was Jimmy just too sick with this cold or was it the big diamond ring Steve gave Margo just too much for him? Margo, she took the ring but said, "I need time to think it over." Steve agreed. But everyone was pleased, mostly Joey. Was he now into money? Tim was pleased but left early too and not with Jimmy. Was he sick too or did he not want Margo to marry? What was up with them?

Merit said to Margo as most people were leaving, "Take my car, it is black, and go talk to Jimmy tonight. I know you are in love with Jimmy. Tell him. It is now or never. I think Jimmy loves you too in a romantic way. Go see him tonight." So Margo did take Merit's car and dressed in black went to the house with no one knowing but Merit. Margo went to Tim's house, and used Merit's keys to get into the house. Then Margo knocked on Jimmy's bedroom door. Jimmy had just taken more cold medication then to bed. He thought it was Merit, so Jimmy didn't answer.

Margo whispered, "Jimmy, it is me, Margo. Can I come into your bedroom? Do I need to see you? Can we talk?" Jimmy got up and checked himself to make sure he was okay for her to see him. He checked his breath to see if it smelled okay. Jimmy let Margo into his bedroom.

As he opened the door, Jimmy said, "Are you alright? Did Steve hurt you? Are you going to marry Steve? Tim and Merit are not here tonight. Are you afraid to be here alone with me? It is very late." Margo walked into Jimmy bedroom then ran her hand up his arm. She pulled herself close to Jimmy, kissing him on the lips long and hard. Jimmy didn't pull away and let her do whatever she wanted to him. They made love for the first time for Margo. Then they went to sleep. After a few hours, Margo got up and tried to get dressed without waking Jimmy. Jimmy woke up as Margo was trying to leave and he said, "Can we please have something to eat this morning and talk?"

Margo replied, "No, I have to get home before Mom finds out I am gone. We can talk later. I love you, Jimmy." Margo was out the door and drove away. Jimmy got up and showered then drove after her. It was still dark when Margo arrived home. She saw someone coming after her from her window, so she got her gun and Merit shot them. Jimmy fell to the ground, and it hurt so much, but he loved her. Merit came running first, and the whole family came out to see what happened.

Merit said, "We thought someone out here, so we called Jimmy. I didn't think he would be here so fast. And I shot the guy outside. Sorry, Jimmy." Jimmy called out Margo's name, but the family was sure Jimmy was just worried about Margo being safe, and they believe Merit's story. The ambulance came to take Jimmy to the hospital. Margo and Merit got in with Jimmy in the back. Margo was crying so hard.

Jimmy took out a banknote and had Margo sign her name as Mrs. Jimmy Elgin just in case he would not be okay. Merit promised to make sure the bank got it first thing. At the hospital, Gerald was there and took Jimmy into surgery to remove the bullet. Joey called all over but could not find Tim anywhere. Margo stayed at the hospital with her family waiting to see if Jimmy would be okay and Merit took the banknote to Jimmy's bank as he promised. Tim came to the hospital and sat by Jimmy as he slept. Everyone else went home, but Margo didn't want to.

Jimmy woke up to hear a thump on the floor, and it was Tim, face down on the floor. Jimmy tried to call the nurse, but no one came, so he got out of bed to help Tim into the other bed. The nurse came in and called for help. Tim was not breathing so the nurse gave Tim mouth to mouth. Tim responded right away, and Gerald came in with help to take Tim away for tests, but Tim cried, "Let the woman do her work. She is not done helping me!"

Gerald replied, "In your dreams, Tim. Jimmy, back in bed." They took Tim away, but after a few hours, Tim was back on the bed beside Jimmy. Gerald gave Tim orders, "You got yourself too run down from all these funerals. But you can't stay in the hospital because you still have a bill from before which is way overdue. I am sorry, but pay your bill."

All Jimmy could think of was that Gerald was too much of a doctor now and that money was his only concern. But Gerald looked at Jimmy and said, "If you have sex with a woman and she shoots you, don't put her on your checking account as your wife. Your new wife has taken all your money out of the bank, and the bank says she had a paper signed with Mrs. Jimmy Elgin."

Marci and George were waiting to see Jimmy and heard it all. George said, "Jimmy, I have been having sex with Marci, and she has never shot me. Maybe we should go over the steps before you try this again. I do agree with Gerald that if a woman shoots you, don't put her on your money bank accounts or marry her. So let's go over this again, you got married last night, had sex, then she shot you, so you put her on your bank account and now she had taken all your money out. You have no money, is that about right? And

Merit with Margo is covering this up for you. All Margo is doing is crying, and I don't believe for a minute Merit shot you."

Marci said, "Come on George, we are going. Jimmy, I am sure she had a very good reason to take the money. Just give her time to explain. Women have issues with money, and sometimes we don't come across as the best in our use of money."

Tim had heard the issue and was laughing, "Jimmy got married and had sex? She shot him and not my son? Merit would lie for Jimmy and so would Margo. Then she took all his money? Jimmy that does sound like your love life. We can't live with women, but we want them, and we can't shoot them. What to do? I am feeling better. Want to talk about it? I am dying to hear." Jimmy just shook his head very sadly, no. Jimmy looked at all the guys that were there in his room, and they had a smile on their faces from ear to ear. Even Joey came in with Sue, looking very surprised.

Sue kissed Jimmy's forehead and said, "Don't worry Jimmy, we'll live through this together too." Then Sue kissed Tim's forehead and just sat there until Merit came to take them both home. Jimmy did not want to talk. Days passed, and Margo came to Jimmy for more money. What could he say? Margo went through her pockets then Jimmy saw the paid receipt for Tim's hospital bill. Merit motioned to Jimmy, thank you, so Tim would not hear it. Jimmy now knew where all his money went to and he should have paid Tim's hospital bill himself, but he didn't.

Merit was taking care of his dad, and Jimmy told Margo how sorry he was that he had not paid Tim's hospital bill before that. Margo said, "That is okay, maybe you did not know about it. Anyway, you were too sick. I hope it was okay that I took your money to pay for it, so Uncle Tim could go to another hospital for help?"

Jimmy kissed Margo and said, "Yes my dear, it was very good that you did that. I love you."

Merit came out of Tim bedroom saying, "A man has to do what a man has to do." And out the door Merit went. Jimmy was not sure, but Merit was always a little different. He did nothing.

Then they went on a plane to a big hospital to get Tim his treatments. Merit with his dad. Jimmy and Margo, together went to help Tim.

Larry found out Tim was sick and was hearing Mr. King's document which left him only one-third of the company he had. Larry was going to fire Tim and give his job to Mr. King's daughter so he would have two-thirds of the company on his side. But where was Larry's partner, Mr. King's son, who also got one-third of the company and money? Mr. King's son did not even come to his father's funeral. Linda called Tim at the hospital as soon as the plane landed to tell him all the news about what Larry was doing. I guess it did pay for Tim to have a romantic affair with his boss's wife. Tim knew Larry was out to get him and that Mr. King's son had died.

Margo went into action and called Steve to buy any shares of that company if it was up for sale. Steve had the money and would do anything for his bride to be, Margo. As Tim thought, Mr. King's son was found at the bottom of the river close to his dad's home by the police at the request of his sister. She was sure her brother would have been at their dad's funeral if he was alive. Now, Mr. King's Will read that if any of his unmarried children died before he did then their one-third of the company and money would be divided up by the employees in this way: all started employees got two shares which was Tim, Joey, Charles, Jim, John. Gerald, Bob, and the two guys that died the time Jimmy went to help Joey with blood. Larry got four shares, bank ten shares, and for all the other new employees to vote on the last two shares for hundred shares. There would be a vote to see who controlled the company.

Steve called Margo back right away and said, "Mr. King's daughter put all her shares up for sale. She doesn't want to work at this company with Larry. I have bought one-third of the company for you, my love." Tim was so pleased, but Jimmy knew if Steve found out about him and Margo, what would Steve do with those shares he just bought? Steve couldn't know.

Jimmy did not want Tim to lose his job this way and all the work Tim had put into that company. Then what about all the money Tim had taken from Larry over the years? Jimmy talked it over with Margo and Merit. They were all in agreement not to tell Steve at this time.

It was to be the first of the year when the Judge would take the vote on who had control of the most shares of the company. Jimmy was counting Tim, Joey, and Gerald each had two votes, so that was six with Steve's thirty-three was thirty-nine for Tim. Larry had his thirty-three and four more than Bob and John's two shares was forty-one shares. It was close and what about Jim and Charles' shares, the two dead guys' families, the bank, and the last two shares? Every vote counted and every share was a vote. When they got back, Steve promised Margo all his shares as a wedding gift to his bride. Tim had Margo set the wedding date as in December. Steve's family was thrilled and gave Margo land which they would pay for, a house built with the complete finishing of furniture for the wedding gift to her. Jimmy was not sure of all this, but he couldn't tell Tim about him and Margo. Tim was too weak from being sick and then all this issue with Larry with his company. But Jimmy knew Margo planned to tell the family at Thanksgiving lunch about them and their love for each other. Jimmy and Margo wanted to marry. Jimmy couldn't tell Margo not to tell her family about them.

The summer came, and it was busy. Jimmy was checking and rechecking the votes. Tim worked on his health. Margo had her home built. Margo made her bedroom with two doors to the hallway, so it looked like two separate rooms. Margo told Tim and Steve she needs Jimmy's bedroom right beside hers for protection. No one went into Margo's bedroom to see it was just one big bedroom for her and Jimmy. Jimmy did not like the idea of living in a house paid for by Steve's family, but he did like sleeping with Margo, so he did it.

On Halloween, Tim had a free big party for all the town's children. The work was almost at a stop with the company, and most employees had so few hours much that no one had money. The college was not paying much because no one knows who would run this company and if there would be jobs. Tim talked to the people and tried to give them hope.

At Thanksgiving, Jimmy prayed in church for an answer to what he believed Margo would be telling her family about them. Jimmy did not know if this was a good enough prayer, but God was his only hope. After church, they went to Sue. They had gotten all the food days before on Sue's list, but now after prayer, Joey asked the question, "What are the sins of the family that I don't know?" Margo started to speak, and Jimmy just closed his eyes. Then Merit spoke up.

Merit said, "Canvas, Charles' daughter and I are having a baby. I want to ask her to marry me."

Tim said, "Yes, do the right thing. Ask the girl to marry you but first, go to her parents and ask them for their blessing on this engagement." Merit agreed.

Jimmy was sure this was not Merit's child. Canvas was a wild girl, and he was sure she had been with many. Jimmy said, "Tim, you should check this Canvas to see if it is Merit's baby." Tim shook his head no. Then Jimmy went to Merit and asked, "Did you do this to stop Margo from telling about us?"

Merit replied, "Yes, in a way. If Steve finds out about you and Margo sleeping together, he will be mad. He may take his shares away, and then my dad would lose. But when my dad was so sick, I asked him what he wanted more than anything in the world, and he said a grandson. So I went out and just did it with Canvas. And now we are going to have a baby. I hope a boy. A man has to do what a man has to do." Jimmy was speechless. Merit was a good friend, a heart of gold, and rocks for brains. Merit did ask that Margo and Steve not get married until after he and Canvas could marry. They did have to marry so Steve put off their wedding until later.

Christmas came, and the family walked in with their heads high. Merit, with his pregnant wife to be, Charles and Penny's daughter. They were so happy about the wedding, and so was Betty. Jimmy and Merit were sure that at least Charles and Jim would divide their shares equally one of Tim and one of Larry. Then Jimmy found out the two families of the dead guys would give Tim their shares because it was Tim who helped their families after the death of the guys, not Larry. So that was four shares from them with two from Charles and Jim. Tim had forty-five to Larry's forty-three. Jimmy was sure the bank would play it safe, five for each.

Then, other employees who all came to that free Halloween party, their shares would go to Tim. So Tim with fifty-two and forty-eight for Larry. Tim would win. But Larry got the Judge to delay the count for another year to be sure so soon after Mr. King's death.

Tim, Jimmy, and Margo's birthday came, and the three best friends went out to eat and enjoy each other. Merit's wedding came, and Jimmy sold his house to pay off the bills from the wedding. Jimmy's housekeeper and her husband were retiring anyway with a nice income Jimmy gave them from the sale of the home. Tim never asked where the money came from, but he did invite the whole town and helped them with new outfits to wear for the wedding and a gift for his son. It was fun for everyone and Betty was home enjoying it all. But that night, Margo's little sick sister, Sally, died. It was a rainy day at the funeral. Merit and Canvas went to Paris with Betty for their honeymoon. Larry was even nice to Tim at the funeral.

The summer was nice, and people were not fighting about anything. Tim went to work as always. Then Merit had his baby, and it was a boy. But the baby was not sick like Merit and Tim. Jimmy knew this was not Merit's son. Jimmy tried to get a DNA test on the baby but Tim wouldn't. And Sue had another baby boy who died right away after birth. The child had all kinds of health issues. Margo and Merit study why? Had the drugs Joey used so long ago still have an issue with his babies? Sue had never done drugs. There were no easy answers.

Halloween came, and Tim had another free party for the town. Jobs were still not there because the question of the company was still not solved. Who would run the company, Tim or Larry?

For Thanksgiving, Tim, Margo, and Jimmy went to get the food on Sue's list. On Jimmy's mind was about Margo telling her family about them. Tim's mind was on the food he wanted Sue to cook for him. Margo said something different as they got the food. Margo said, "Don't get so much frozen food. The freezer is full of Dad."

Jimmy stopped and looked at Margo. She was not laughing, so Jimmy took Tim with the turkey in Tim's hand to the check out with Margo then to the car they went. Tim asked, "What about the little buns and cream pies?" Jimmy looked sick, did he hear Margo right?

Margo repeated it, "We can't have much frozen stuff. There is no room in the freezer. We put Dad there."

Tim asked, "You put my brother in the freezer? Why?" Tim was upset and afraid to ask more.

Margo answered, "Merit said he would start to smell if we didn't. Mark thought Mom would be upset if we throw him out. Jr. Joey did not want him stinking up the barn. No one wanted to dig a hole. I should have told someone at the time."

Jimmy said in disbelief, "We will drive out and look. Margo can show us." Margo showed them the freezer and Joey was in it. It looked like Joey had a heart attack. They didn't kill him. Tim just sat on the floor with some cooking sherry and drank it all up. Jimmy called Gerald, and then he prayed. Margo said nothing, not even a tear for Joey, her father.

Gerald came out and looked at Joey then he said, "Who are you people? Why did they not call someone when this happened?"

Jimmy replied, "Maybe they were all in shock. Please help me. Margo and Merit are studying to be doctors, so they knew he died." Sue continued walking around cooking for Thanksgiving as if nothing was wrong.

Jimmy and Gerald did the paperwork and wrote the cause of death as a heart attack. Gerald was okay with helping Jimmy out, but he did say, "This family needs help. Margo and Merit should have known better and called it in." Jimmy nodded in agreement so Gerald would sign the paper that Joey died today and get him ready to be buried. Gerald stamped the paperwork that date and no more was said. Gerald never liked Joey anyway as he believed that Joey was sleeping with his wife, Shirley. The little girl at the church school that Margo hit in the mouth so many years ago was Gerald's oldest daughter who told her about her mom and Margo's dad. But now Margo and Gerald's two daughters were the best of friends.

Jr. Joey had his father's share, and Jimmy was sure Jr. Joey would vote for Larry because he loved working for Larry. Jimmy talked to Sue about it as soon as Joey's funeral was over and Sue demanded Jr. Joey vote his dad's shares for Tim, and so Jr. Joey would or lose this right. Larry was very nice to Tim at Joey's funeral, and Jimmy hoped this silly fight was over. But then Larry found out Linda told Tim everything, so he threw her out of his house and was going to divorce her. Linda moved in with Sue to help her with Joey's death. Charles' son married Larry's daughter. Tim now knew Merit's baby was not his but Tim could not say anything or a loss of vote maybe.

Thanksgiving went on as always with no one noticing Joey was not there Jimmy was happy no one asked the question about the sin of the family this year. And Steve had to wait again for Margo and his wedding because of the death of Margo's father. Jimmy did notice Jr. Joey was married and had a few kids. Jimmy tried to remember when did this all happen. Well, it must have happened one of those summers and Margo came home from college for the wedding. Oh yes, Jimmy remembers now he just loved Margo in her bridesmaid dress. Jimmy couldn't take his eyes off of her. But she was not twenty-one years old then.

Christmas, they all walked in church heads held high and sat in the front row. Linda was with them now and sitting between Tim and Sue. Jimmy just sat with Margo and Steve on the other side of Margo. What was he going to do about Steve? He was a nice guy and a friend. New Years came, and Larry was too calm, what did he know that they didn't? Tim was talking to the police. Tim came over to Jimmy saying, "Gerald has been in a car accident, he died. In his memory and for Jimmy, his best friend we can't vote tonight. Please go home and pray for Gerald Doginmeier's family on this sad night." Jimmy was in shocked. Tim took him home.

Everyone left, but Larry tried to get people to stay and vote. Larry told everyone Gerald's wife Shirley could vote for Gerald, but no one stayed. Larry went to the Judge to get the vote done, but the Judge ruled a six-month wait. Gerald's funeral and Will needed to be read. Jimmy tried to talk to Gerald's widow to see when the funeral was but she told their daughter that she wanted to bury Gerald in the backyard. Jimmy was upset about this and Margo called his daughters. Jimmy and Margo went out to Gerald's home to see the girls, and they were crying over the car accident that took their father's life. The police report said Gerald was driving drunk and hit a steel beam on the bridge. Jimmy did not believe it, but Gerald did drink a lot.

Jimmy asked Gerald's daughters, "Do you need me to pay for your dad's funeral. I will just go with Margo and pick out what you want for it." So the girls and Margo did that, and Jimmy paid for it all himself. The funeral was very nice, and the whole town came. Shirley and Larry laughed through it all, so the girls cried. Tim was sad, but there was nothing he could do. Jimmy took the girls to Gerald's lawyer and guess what? Gerald left everything to his daughters and nothing to his wife. Gerald's daughters gave their father's votes to Tim. Larry and Shirley were not laughing anymore.

Tim, Jimmy, and Margo had their birthdays again with just the three best friends having fun. Steve was not pleased, but Margo explained Jimmy had just lost a best friend and needed her. Larry's divorce came to court and Tim could prove with doctor notes from Gerald's files that Larry had abused Linda for years, until Tim made him stop with Larry's mother and Mr. King. Linda got half of everything which was Larry's shares in the company. Larry got seventeen and his four which left Linda sixteen shares or votes which she was voting for Tim.

So that summer, Tim won, he had sixty-eight shares, and Larry had thirty-two. The problem was over, Tim and Margo owned the company. But Tim said, "We could not have done it without you Jimmy, so the new company is, TMJ." Steve gave Margo his share and the wedding day was set for Christmas because Margo wanted time to plan it right. Steve agreed, but he was a little upset.

The summer was hard, working out the new plans, and Larry's son and daughter were breaking in the company to cause damage to the equipment. Tim had the police help. Then things got bad and Merit's wife, Canvas died in one of the machines. It was not good, and Merit cried. Jimmy asked, "What was Canvas doing at the company?"

Merit replied, "I had Margo give her a job." Margo agreed she did and let Canvas try different things at the company. Jimmy looked at Tim, and he just looked down.

Then Jimmy spoke, "If I am part of this company than employees all have to be trained before they can do any work at the company." Tim and Margo quickly agreed, and it was a rule.

Canvas's funeral was sad, and Tim took the little boy to her parents' place to care for him. Tim said, "My son, Merit just can't care for the child without your daughter." Canvas's parents agreed to care for the little boy, and it made them feel better to have a part of their daughter with them. Tim never told Canvas's parents that Merit was not the father.

Jimmy worked hard to find out who did this and some DNA was on the site and Canvas's body. It was Larry's son, Lawrence and Bobby Jameson. As they looked for evidence, Jimmy also found a gun in Jim Jameson's house which matched the gun and bullets used to kill Mr. King's first wife and Tim's sister, Annie. To the court, they went, and Karen, Jimmy's wife, was found guilty. Karen got the death penalty, unlike Lawrence and Bobby who got life in jail for the death of Canvas. That could have been unintentional.

Larry asked for a meeting of peace with Tim alone in a place out where no one could find them. Jimmy was going with Tim; he did not trust Larry. Margo and Steve would wait by the road entries. Tim took the meeting hoping to learn more about his sister's death and his mom's. Jimmy was sure Larry was behind it, but Karen would not tell about why she shot both women.

Tim and Jimmy waited for Larry at the meeting place until they heard gunshots. Jimmy in a flash was down to Margo. Steve said, "I saw nothing, Margo had to have something from the car down the other side of this hill and when I got back they were shot." Jimmy called the police before anyone moved. Larry and his lawyer, Bob were killed by gunshots to the heads. There were drugs in the car and a lot of money. Jimmy was sure that the evidence showed three guys, but only found two dead. Margo cried uncontrollably. Jimmy had Steve take Margo home. The police thought it was a drug deal that went wrong and Larry was trying to frame Tim with the drugs or kill Tim over the loss of the company. Jimmy called Marci to see if she knew anything. Had Margo asked her for help? Marci didn't answer any of Jimmy's questions which was not like Marci. The third guy was to kill Tim? There was not the time to go over it because Loretta, Larry's daughter, blamed Tim, Jimmy, and Margo for her father's death. Bob's children also threatened Tim, Jimmy, and Margo to get revenge for their father's death. Steve was on for the wedding which Margo had done nothing to plan.

Steve's parents had their wedding anniversary and wanted to have them all go out to eat at their favorite place. Jimmy made some ice tea, which he did not really like but knew Steve's mom loved ice tea. As they came to the house Margo had built with their money, they sat with the ice tea waiting for Margo to come down from her bedroom dressed to go. Steve said, "I will go up and see what is taking Margo so long. Maybe I can help hurry her along." So Steve left, and they waited longer. Jimmy poured the ice tea for everyone to drink. Then Jimmy took a big mouthful of the sweet tea.

Steve's mother said, "Maybe they are making me a grandchild up there." And all the ice tea came out of Jimmy's mouth. It went all over Steve's mom's pretty new dress.

Tim called out to Margo, "Margo, Jimmy spit all over your future mother-in-law. Boy, Jimmy, are you in trouble now. You are going to get it from Margo." Jimmy tried to help clean Steve's mother up, but her dress was a mess.

Margo came down with Steve, and said, "Steve, take your mother home and clean her up. Tim, you and Steve's dad go to the café and save the table for us. Just drink something. Jimmy, in the kitchen, now." Tim was laughing and making fun of Jimmy who was in trouble now.

In the kitchen, Jimmy went and waited for Margo. What could he say? They left, and Margo came into the kitchen and said, "Jimmy, on the table." Jimmy sat on the table, and Margo walked over to him and started to make love to him. Well, Jimmy was not the kind of guy to have sex on a kitchen table, but he couldn't stop. Then Merit walked into the kitchen and Margo screamed at him, "Get out now."

Merit kept on walking and replied, "I am never eating on the table again." After the passion on the table they went up to the bedroom, and Margo called Tim, telling him she was not coming because of what had happened. Margo was staying home with Jimmy. Tim took that as Jimmy was in big trouble and not that Jimmy had just gotten great sex from Margo.

Jimmy and Tim were worried about Margo being safe with all the threats from Larry and Bob's kids. Steve agreed it must be upsetting Margo for she was sick a lot, mostly in the mornings. So Steve's family had a place that no one knew about, and Margo to Jimmy's surprise, agreed to stay there with protection. Jimmy used the people where Marci and him had a home to protect. Jimmy asked Tim, "Please check Margo out, she is sick almost every day. I am worried."

Tim said, "Margo has agreed to make an appointment for a complete physical next week."

Jimmy went to see Margo every day, and she was sleeping a lot. Then Margo asked Jimmy to come and eat with her one night just the two of them. Jimmy was pleased; they could talk.

At the company, things were going better, so Jimmy left Tim and went to see Margo that night. Margo had a nice table set with candlelight and all Jimmy's favorite foods. Margo was a good cook like her mother, Sue. After prayer and they ate, Margo said, as she looked into Jimmy's eyes, "You are going to be a father. I am pregnant. Remember the table sex?"

Jimmy was very surprised but pleased and kissed Margo, saying, "I love you so much. Marry me. I will tell Steve in the morning about us. I am sure I can get him to understand." Margo said nothing, and to bed, they went. In the morning, Jimmy got up early, and he went to see Steve.

Now, here is a little advice for anyone doing something like this. Never tell a guy that you have just got the love of his life pregnant with your child if he has gun in the house. Very bad idea. Trust it, he will not understand and will try to kill you. Margo awoke thinking just that and called Tim to go to Steve's house to help Jimmy.

Jimmy got to Steve's place and asked, "Could we talk?" Steve sat down to listen to what Jimmy had to say. Jimmy continued, "Margo and I are in love. She is having my baby and can't marry you. I am very sorry. I know we were friends, but the love is just too strong for us to stop." Steve said nothing but got up and went for his gun and started shooting at Jimmy. Jimmy hid behind the furniture, but Steve kept shooting. Then Tim walked in without a gun and Steve shoot Tim. Jimmy threw himself over Tim as Steve continued to shoot at them. Margo walked in next, and Steve lowered his gun just long enough for Margo to shoot Steve in the head. Tears came down Steve's eyes as he fell to the floor from the bullet that sent him to his death.

Margo called the ambulance and started to care for Tim and Jimmy. Jimmy replied, "Help Tim, I am okay." But Jimmy was not okay, he was shot many times, and then Jimmy didn't talk anymore. Jimmy was the worst and Tim would be okay. Tim kept Jimmy in sleep so he would not die from the pain. No one knew what happened and Margo was not talking. Mark and Merit helped Margo.

Merit said, "That Larry's daughter had tried to find Margo to kill her and Steve tried to stop her and her friends. Then Jimmy came, but they had killed Steve because he would not tell them where Margo was. Jimmy was shooting it out with them, and Tim came, so they shot him. Margo came when it was all over, and she called for help as they ran away. Jimmy was trying to save Steve's life. No one questioned Merit's story, and everyone believed the baby was Steve's that Margo was having so Steve's parents gave Margo all the money from Steve's life insurance. They also put their business in Margo and the unborn baby's name. Tim was to help manage it. Steve's parents worried about Jimmy, the man they thought was trying to save their son with his own life. Mark knew this was not true, but he kept his mouth shut for the money.

Christmas came, their birthdays, and Easter, then the baby was born a little girl, May 31. Jimmy was still in a coma. But Margo went into labor in his room, so Tim delivered the baby there. As Tim worked with Margo, he laid the baby girl on Jimmy's chest. That was the start of a friendship the baby girl had with Jimmy. Margo named the girl, Sarah Sue Elgin because she was not married to anyone at the time of the birth of her baby. Margo would not leave the house to go anywhere. Tim, Mark, and Merit had to do everything. Steve's parents were very nice to Margo and just thought Margo missed their son, Steve, as they did. Margo had Tim and Linda be Sarah's Godparents. Marci and George came to help Margo with Jimmy and Sarah.

Then one day without warning, Jimmy just woke up and started asking questions. Sarah was in the bedroom with him, and so was Margo. Margo cried, "Tim, come here now; Jimmy is awake." Tim ran to the room.

Jimmy's memory was gone, but Tim was sure it would come back slowly. Tim set up a program to help Jimmy remember things slowly. Jimmy had to use a cane to walk, and he had all kinds of questions, but he loved the baby girl, Sarah, right from the start. For the first time, Margo left the house to go to church with Jimmy and baby Sarah. The pastor had been coming to the house for all their church needs. Tim told Merit and Mark his idea which was, "I think Jimmy and Margo should get married, so Sarah has a daddy."

Merit and Mark agreed that was a good idea and now Tim needed to tell Jimmy so they did not have to do so much work around the place. Margo was impossible when she was pregnant.

For Halloween, Jimmy took little Sarah trick and treating even if she was just a baby of about six months. Tim and Margo watched from the car laughing. Merit and Mark still did the free Halloween party for the town even if they lived out of town. Tim talked to Jimmy about him marrying Margo so Sarah would have a daddy. Even Steve's parents went to Jimmy about that they were so sure their son, Steve would want him to marry Margo, so Sarah had a loving dad. No one knew but Merit did, and he was telling no one because he was Margo friend or what?

After Thanksgiving lunch, which was all of Jimmy's favorites, Jimmy took Margo out to the garden filled with red roses and got down on one knee to ask, "I love you and Sarah, will you marry me?" Then Jimmy took out a big diamond ring and put it on Margo's ring finger.

Margo cried. "Yes, oh yes, I love you too." Margo threw her arms around him, and they kissed.

Everyone was happy but Jr. Joey said, "You will never marry my sister, you animal." Then he and Jenny walked out the door. The kids were playing, so Merit was to take them home later. Mark agreed that would be best. But on the way home, Jr. Joey and Jenny got into a bad car accident, and were killed. Mark and Merit took their kids to live with Jenny's cousin where Tim did not understand. The funeral was very sad, and their children were there, Sue couldn't understand.

Margo started to plan her wedding with Jimmy, and she wanted it to be on Valentines Day.

Christmas came, and Jimmy was so pleased to have Sarah's first Christmas and they enjoyed that completely. The new year was a new start to all the hurt they were leaving behind. Margo went out to find a wedding dress with Sue and Linda. Jimmy was watching

Sarah with Tim, Merit, and Mark. When suddenly, with no warning, Sarah had little gold like antenna coming out of her head. She disappeared from one area then reappeared in another. Jimmy went after her. Tim just left. After Jimmy found Sarah, Merit and Mark watched her with a baby promise from Sarah not to do that again until he came back with great Uncle Tim.

Jimmy found Tim in a bar, drunk. Jimmy tried to talk with Tim, but Tim just hit Jimmy across his face. Jimmy did nothing, letting Tim hit him because Jimmy now knew Sarah was his daughter. Jimmy's memory was coming back to him all at once.

The bar owner called Jim and Charles, they came to stop Tim from hitting Jimmy. But Jimmy's face was now full of blood. Jimmy went to wash his face and then seen how bad it looked. So Jimmy went to sleep in the basement of Margo's house. He didn't want to scare Margo or Sarah. Tim got home. Merit and Mark told Margo all about it. Margo could not find Jimmy. But little Sarah with her special abilities found her daddy and gave him medication for his face which did heal nicely.

After about a week, Margo followed Sarah and found Jimmy hiding in the basement. Margo kissed his face and Tim told Jimmy how sorry he was. Tim agreed to go to AA group meetings to stop drinking forever. Tim said, "I am an alcoholic." The wedding was still on. Margo was very mad at Tim, but if he went to his meetings, she would forgive him.

Jimmy wanted to do something nice for Margo, so he asked her for a date anywhere she wanted to go. Margo replied, "I want you to take me to the movies as our first date." Jimmy agreed. At the movies, Jimmy and Margo sat down, and I think there is a song like this sad movies always make me cry. But the song was about a girl who sees her boyfriend with her best friend, but this was Margo seeing Tim walk in with Linda. Tim was supposed to be at his AA meeting, but there they sat in front of Jimmy and Margo. Tim did kiss Linda, and Margo stood up to make a scene. Then Margo walked out of the movies, and Jimmy followed her.

Margo had all kinds of questions, and Jimmy answered all of them truthfully. Then Margo called Tim's wife, Betty in Paris, France and she was going to divorce Tim. When Tim got home, Jimmy told him the issue, and Tim sold his family home to Jimmy for one dollar. Tim sold Jimmy all his shares in the company. That money he left to Merit and his sister, Mary. Tim never told anyone that Betty had cheated on him first, but Jimmy did tell Margo all about what Betty did to Tim before. Jimmy tried to get Tim to fight for something in the divorce but Tim didn't, he let her have everything. Tim's daughter, Mary, would not even talk to Tim, but Merit was nice to both of his parents. Betty and Mary went back to Paris, France to live and never seen Tim again.

The divorce was bad, and Betty got everything but Tim's parents' home and the company's shares. Tim agreed to everything Betty wanted and said she was right he was the bad guy. Tim now had to live with Margo and had not a penny to his name, but Tim was okay with that. Tim planned not to have any money of his own in his name so Betty couldn't take him back to court. Jimmy could not understand this anger Betty had for Tim when she had done the same thing to him, and she knew it. Jimmy was sure Betty had many boyfriends in Paris, France throughout Tim and her marriage. But that didn't matter to Betty, just what Tim had done to her with Linda. What was it, because it was Linda or women are different? Jimmy could not see it, but he would learn the hard way about women.

Tim said, "It is always best to give them what they want in a divorce until it hurts so much you think you will die but it is just safer to do that. Trust me; I know women. They will hurt you until you die otherwise. It is just money, and our kids are old enough to be on their own."

Margo was still mad at Tim, but she agreed to let him walk her down the aisle to marry Jimmy. Merit was paying for Margo's wedding, was this with the money Tim left him? Well, yes and no. Merit also got money from Marci and George for Margo's big costly wedding to Jimmy. Jimmy did not want to say anything, he wanted Margo to have the wedding of her dreams.

On the wedding day, Tim came to talk to Jimmy. Tim said, "My best friend is getting married. I always told you this would happen one day. I know you love Margo very much and will be a great father to Sarah. But be sure to have more children." Jimmy just laughed.

Then Tim went to Margo; he said, "Be good to Jimmy. He is my best friend in the whole world. Love him and never hurt him. He loves you so much. Always remember that. Don't hurt Jimmy because that would kill me." Then Tim gave his arm to Margo. Sue and Tim walked Margo down that old church's aisle to Jimmy waiting to marry her. The wedding in black, white, and red so pretty. The whole town was there, all the employees, and all of the people that lived where Marci was. Sarah was the flower girl with Merit and Mark the best men and Gerald's daughters the bridesmaids. Marci and George sang the wedding songs.

For the honeymoon, Jimmy and Margo went on a trip around the world. They took Tim and little Sarah with them. Jimmy loved the Maya temples in Mexico. Tim loved Germany and looked up the camps where Hitler killed so many Jews. Margo was sick most of the time from their wedding night. Sarah loved everything but most of all her parents together. They came back on Margo birthday and rested a lot. Merit and Mark ran the company.

Easter morning came, and Sarah loved church and finding Easter eggs, but Margo took Jimmy aside and said, "You are going to be a father again." Jimmy was so happy all he did was kiss her.

Tim was happy too. What could go wrong anymore? All was good in their world.

Tim married Linda in a small wedding just with Jimmy, Margo, Sarah, Merit, Mark, and Sue. No one else.

Sarah had her birthday, and it was at Marci's place. Tim must have sat on something red because Tim whispered to Jimmy, "I think I have my woman's thing. See red blood on my pant. Come to see in the bathroom. Check me." Jimmy shook his head no.

Then Tim went to Margo and Margo said, "Bend over and drop your pants." Margo put on some plastic gloves, and her figure nails were very long, so they made a sound popping through the plastic gloves. They all hear the unbelievable cry from Tim of pain as Margo check. Jimmy just closed his eyes as Margo came out saying, "Just bleeding hemorrhoid." No one said any more about it, but Tim wanted to go home, so Jimmy took him home but first they got a pillow with a hole in the middle for Tim to sit on. Tim was in real pain now. Jimmy stayed with Tim but couldn't help him in any way. Margo had to be his doctor in this situation. And Merit was not the smartest guy on the block even as a doctor. He had a good heart, but that was all.

When Margo got home, she said to Jimmy, "I need to tell you sometime; please sit down." Jimmy was now afraid, what could Margo have to say that he needed to sit down, but he did as told. Margo had already told him they were having another baby. Margo said, "We are having twins. You know I am a twin. Are you okay?" Jimmy just cried with joy, and they kissed.

After that, Margo became impossible to be around. She was not nice to anyone in the house but Tim. I guess a woman is always nice to her doctor. Jimmy got the worst of it. Margo wanted ice cream and vanilla. When Jimmy came with the vanilla ice cream, she cried she wanted strawberry. Jimmy started to write it down what Margo asked for but that was not useful because she always changed her mind.

Merit said, "This time Mr. Jimmy, you have to take care of your pregnant wife. Last time I had to care for her while you were sleeping. You do the crime; you pay the price, not me." It was so bad Jimmy told Margo he would have a new house built just the way she wanted it and that did help. Margo was very bossy to the poor builder, and she did stay out of the company which all the employees would hide when Margo came to work. Merit and Mark even helped pay for the new house to keep Margo away from the company. But Jimmy had to double then triple the workers' pay, and they worked mostly at night when Margo was sleeping with Jimmy.

One night, Jimmy woke up to see Margo with a knife over him. Tim grabbed the knife, and they prayed hard for those babies to come out of Margo soon. Their prayers answered, and Margo cried to Jimmy, "The babies are coming out now." Jimmy went into action and got Margo into the car with Merit to watch Sarah, then to the hospital, they went. Margo said to Jimmy, "Are you planning to deliver these babies yourself?" Jimmy turned the car around and went back to get Tim out of bed with coffee in Tim's hand they left again for the hospital. Margo was crying in pain and Jimmy went to kiss her, but Margo hit Jimmy in the eye, and he had a black eye.

Tim said to Jimmy, "Stay away from hitting areas for women can be not nice at this time to their husbands. It is just the pain and not you or the babies." Jimmy did, and his son was born first, who Jimmy named Michael Joey Elgin. The girl came next, and Jimmy named her Tammy Margo Elgin. Margo was all smiles now and loved Jimmy so much. Sarah just loved the babies.

After Margo got back to her old self, they started to move into the new house. Jimmy hated moving, so he took the kids with him to work and turned the millions of dollars from the money Steve's family left Margo into billions of dollars in work at the company. They got all new furniture, but Margo wanted the kitchen table from the old house. Merit and Mark were glad she took it because they were going to live in Margo's old house with her mother, Sue. Sue had not been the same since Margo's dad died and she needed care. Tim and Linda went to live with Jimmy, Margo, and the kids in their new home Jimmy had built just for them. All was good, but now they needed more workers for the company and Margo didn't want Jimmy talking to most of the employees, so they needed top guys to work that Margo approved.

CHAPTER FOUR

THE GUYS, T-JAY PEDERSON, SAM ELGIN, AND MICKEY JOHNSON

T-Jay had just graduated from the university in trade. His father was into imports and exports. It was almost September, and with summer classes T-Jay would graduate. He didn't want the graduation ceremony, just some time to see the world. But his father said, "No, you need to come and work with me now, my way." T-Jay's mom always agreed with his dad; she loved him so much. T-Jay was an only child, and his dad hated guys in white suits, so T-Jay started wearing white suits all the time. Different color white but still white is all he wore.

T-Jay and his father were disagreeing again when T-Jay just walked out the door and drove away. T-Jay thought what could he do? Now let me stop here and say one thing, "If you have everything and now just walk away, who do you think is paying for all you had?" T-Jay found out when his credit cards stopped working, his cash ran out and the bank explained to him the money in there was his fathers, not his. What his father had to do was cut him off. T-Jay was without money, and as he came out of the bank in this nowhere town, someone was taking his car away. T-Jay said, "Hey! What are you doing? That's my car."

The man stopped and handed T-Jay a paper which read he needed to pay the car off himself which was over fifty thousand dollars. The guy said, "Pay the bill or shut your spoiled mouth, kid. I'll let you think about it while I eat. If you can come up with the money when I come out then good, otherwise the car is with me." The guy went into the cafe. T-Jay thought, who would give him fifty thousand dollars? Who could he call? Well, T-Jay did not work and play well with others. He never had a best friend. So, T-Jay sat there thinking, and he was hungry. Then, out of nowhere came this guy who sat down beside T-Jay. They just sat there as the guy studied T-Jay's situation and knew what was going on. T-Jay was sure he didn't know this guy.

Then the guy spoke, "I am Jimmy Elgin. It looks like you could use some help. Maybe call your parents, need cash?"

T-Jay answered, "Yes, but I will never call my dad for money. I can work it off if you have something I can do?"

Jimmy replied, "Yes, I do need someone to help me with this company. Tell me about yourself." T-Jay made it short and quick, his education and lack of experience. Jimmy just got up and paid the man for T-Jay's car, fifty thousand dollars in cash.

T-Jay said, "Should you be carrying that much cash out here?" Jimmy did not answer but put gas in the car and paid for that too. T-Jay continued, "Thank you, but now who do I have to kill?" Jimmy just smiled and got into T-Jay's car.

Then Jimmy said, "Here are the papers on your car. Give me a ride home, okay? I have walked a little too far, and I don't feel like walking back. I need help with my job. I need someone to import things that I need for building what I need to build, then export it when I am done building it to where it needs to go. Want the job? Come to meet my family, and we can eat something." They drove up to a beautiful big castle which was where Jimmy directed T-Jay to drive. The prettiest woman T-Jay had ever seen came running out to Jimmy with a guy at her side. Jimmy got out of the car when she hugged and kissed him all over.

Jimmy said, "I am sorry. I promise I will never do that again. Can we get something to eat? T-Jay, my wife, Margo and honey I would like T-Jay to work with us."

The woman said, "Anything you want, Jimmy." The guy looked T-Jay over, and so did some white-haired people.

In the house, they went, and the guy said, "My name is Tim Elgin. These are Jimmy's children. My wife's name is Linda." The little blonde girl who T-Jay could not believe could even talk came over to him.

She said, "My name is Sarah, this is my brother Michael and my sister, Tammy." Then Sarah put her little hand out for T-Jay to shake and he did. T-Jay looked around, and the house was very special and nice. Tim was dancing and so was Sarah, then Jimmy handed Tim money.

Tim and Linda left. Jimmy sat by his kids and asked T-Jay more questions about what he thought on imports and exports. T-Jay was so pleased because no one ever asked him about anything he thought. T-Jay had all kinds of ideas on work. Jimmy even wrote some down with a few questions on what T-Jay meant by that idea. What would this way of doing it service? Jimmy was hard for T-Jay to understand and he was speaking English so Margo would repeat it in a simpler term then T-Jay could answer Jimmy.

Tim came in with pizza and sang, "Pizza, pizza, who wants pizza? It is pizza night." The kids came to the table, and Jimmy helped his kids get ready for pizza. Margo helped Linda with the drinks. There were very nice dishes on the table with a knife, fork, and cloth napkins, but Jimmy used his figures to get the pizza out for his kids. Tim said, "We have to wait for the kids to get their pizza first, then we pray, and we can get our pizza."

There was one box on the table, but T-Jay had seen Tim bring in at least five extra-large pizzas. Each child got their pizza, and then Jimmy said the prayer which Tim tried to copy the hand thing but got it all wrong. Jimmy got another box of pizza from the kitchen where they were keeping it hot. Two guys came, and Tim said, "This is my son, Merit and Margo's twin brother Mark. Sit down with us you guys and have some pizza." Merit and Mark went into the kitchen and got their pizza; they looked funny at the wooden table where Tim and the others were eating. Merit and Mark ate their pizza in the living room. Tim said, "Don't make a mess in there. Jimmy, tell them they have to eat here." Jimmy got all red in his face but said nothing. Tim and Linda looked confused. Then Merit and Mark left. Tim called after them, "Wait to take T-Jay with you."

Jimmy spoke up right away and said, "No, T-Jay can stay here tonight. We'll get him a place in the morning. I have more questions about imports and exports." T-Jay was pleased he didn't have to go with those two guys for the night.

T-Jay got a room to stay the night, and Jimmy put his twins to bed. Little Sarah brought out a book for T-Jay to read to her, so he did. Then Margo came and took her to bed with Jimmy. Then Jimmy came out to ask T-Jay more questions about this work. Jimmy wanted the stuff to get there, but he didn't want to have to think about how it happened. Jimmy just wanted to do the work and not the shipping of anything. Margo called Jimmy to bed, and he went to their room. Tim called out from his bedroom, "Remember about the sounds of Jimmy? Are you going to sleep or bed with Margo?"

Jimmy called back to Tim, "Your bedroom is way over there. You can't hear anything from here. Go to sleep with your wife."

Tim called back, "That is why I am complaining. I can't hear a thing way over here. How can I improve my sex life if I can't hear you to learn and what about T-Jay? His bedroom is way over there too. How is a guy to learn?"

Jimmy said, "Tim, you know I don't like that kind of talk. T-Jay is here to learn the company and work." Jimmy went to bed, closing his door. T-Jay looked out his door and saw the white-haired people cleaning the house very quietly.

In the morning, Jimmy was making his kids' breakfast, pancakes. Tim sat at the table too. But no Margo. T-Jay asked Jimmy, "Who are all those white-haired people? Do they work for you?"

Jimmy replied, "Yes, but they also do security as well as cleaning." Jimmy looked at Tim saying, "The next thing we need is more security for my family. Vicki is just not working out." Tim nodded in agreement, and they prayed. Margo came out half dressed, eating off of Jimmy's plate. Tim just looked down, so T-Jay did the same. T-Jay was sure Jimmy would tell her to put clothes on, but he didn't, he just watched if Tim or T-Jay looked at his pretty wife. They didn't.

Margo said, "I think we need security around Jimmy and not just the kids with me.

We need this as soon as possible. What about the guy who we helped get through law enforcement college? When does he graduate?"

Tim replied, "In May. But no security for me? Am I not important?" Everyone was laughing, even the kids. They all took their plates into the kitchen for Jimmy to put in the dishwasher while Margo finished dressing to go to work. Tim carried his plate very carefully, so T-Jay did too. They found T-Jay a place to live that day on the phone and then to work they went which was fun for T-Jay. Jimmy was going to train T-Jay at the company, and Jimmy knew everything.

T-Jay went to the apartment place alone, and it was very nice. Jimmy had paid for the place with any changes T-Jay wanted and furniture. T-Jay went shopping. It was Saturday, and Jimmy would be home for family time. T-Jay also needed it all in white. He got all white furniture and even rugs. Then T-Jay went to buy more white suits. When T-Jay got back to his apartment, it was all done. The white-haired people were leaving.

In the morning, T-Jay found the local church and Jimmy with his family was there. Jimmy motioned for T-Jay to sit with them and he did, by little Sarah who wanted him to sit by her. After church, T-Jay had lunch at Jimmy's home with his family, and he met Vicki. If Vicki were the only woman on the planet, T-Jay would be alone. He did not like Vicki at all, not his type and T-Jay understood how Jimmy could not stand Vicki. Now Margo was good with Vicki, maybe because Jimmy wasn't.

Jimmy said to T-Jay, "You are not here to marry Vicki and get her out of my life are you? I know I can't stand her either but what to do with her? I need security, and she is a woman with my pretty wife and kids. I need a married guy."

T-Jay was sure Jimmy had no problems in hiring a woman to do any job, but he did was want the person to do their job, and all Vicki did was file her nails. Tim laughed. Margo said, "Watch your temper, Jimmy, I am okay with her." T-Jay was very sure that the reason Margo was so okay with Vicki was that Jimmy couldn't stand her. T-Jay had noticed that Jimmy never talked to any of the employees except Merit, Mark, Tim, or Margo. Jimmy did the work, and those four others told everyone else what to do. T-Jay had not been there long, but he was sure Margo was taking no chances of losing her man who kept her in diamond to wear for work and home which was more like a castle. Jimmy a genius, Margo the beauty and Tim was fun.

The twins had their birthday, and the family was there with white-haired people and T-Jay. On Halloween Jimmy wanted to take the kids trick or treating. Margo wanted T-Jay to be security for Jimmy. She liked that T-Jay was with Jimmy all the time because he was training T-Jay at the company. Merit and Mark were with Jimmy too. Tim and Margo waited in the car, or we should say what it was a limo. Tim got chocolate all over himself and Merit had to clean up his dad. Tim was a big kid, and though T-Jay didn't like children, Sarah was so grown up in what she did. And the twin was always good. T-Jay liked Jimmy and Margo's kids but Tim not so much.

Thanksgiving came, and they all went to church then a great meal at Jimmy's home. Margo was a very good cook. Christmas came, and Jimmy asked, "Are you going home for the holidays? You should go just this one time, okay?" T-Jay had started to never say no to Jimmy, so he agreed. T-Jay had also learned that the employees love to gossip about their bosses in the bathroom and T-Jay overheard why Merit and Mark would never eat on the wooden table in Jimmy's home. It happened that Jimmy and Margo had sex on that table and Merit saw them then, nine months later Sarah was born. So T-Jay decided to get a nice tablecloth for his nice boss for Christmas. T-Jay gave the tablecloth then left for his parents' place. Which he didn't enjoy, and so he left.

T-Jay's parents were pleased that he got this great job, working for the company and that this boss sent them a beautiful plant for Christmas. T-Jay had also got a very nice Christmas bonus.

When T-Jay got back, the first thing he noticed was the tablecloth he got them for Christmas was on the wooden table. Jimmy said, "Thank you for the nice tablecloth." But Merit and Mark still wouldn't eat on that table. They did look at the tablecloth and smiled but there was no eating there.

New Years, Valentines Day, their birthdays, and Easter with family and the white-haired people at Jimmy's home. Then there was a funeral that just Jimmy and Tim went too. Jimmy had asked T-Jay to stay and make sure Margo and his kids were safe. Margo walked back and forth all the time Jimmy and Tim were gone. When they got back, Margo needed Jimmy all to herself. Then things got back to moral. T-Jay's training with Jimmy finished. T-Jay knew he would never leave this job. But T-Jay was alone a lot and didn't like Merit or Mark. They both tried hard to do whatever Jimmy wanted, but Merit or Mark were not that smart.

T-Jay had just come out of the store from buying more white suits when an old pickup truck hit his white sports car. T-Jay looked to see why and the guy was watching Vicki walking down the street. The guy got out of his pickup and was talking fast about his insurance and how sorry he was. Then the guy said, "My name is Sam Elgin. Is that your girlfriend? I know my insurance will cover all this damage to your white sports car."

T-Jay smiled, he was thinking about how happy Jimmy would be to marry Vicki off to anyone, so he said, "No, she is all yours. I am T-Jay and don't worry about the car; they will get me another one. Why are you in town? Can you give me a ride to my workplace?"

Sam answered, "Yes, I am here to see two guys who had given my family so much after my father died and I promised my mother this past month when she died that I would look them up and somehow repay them." Sam was worried T-Jay would get oil or some dirt from the seat of the old pick-up truck he drove, and he tried to clean the seat, but T-Jay sat there.

To a big blue glass building they went and parked in a parking lot with sports cars. Sam's pick-up truck stood out like it didn't belong there. Into the building they went. The girl at the desk flirted with T-Jay, but he didn't even look at her. Sam said. "Not your type?"

T-Jay replied, "No, too much war paint. I like girls but not the makeup type." And to an office, they went with a guy sleeping on the desk. They sat down in big black leather chairs. Tim woke up and looked at them; he was one of the guys who helped Sam's family.

Tim said, "Was I snoring? Jimmy, T-Jay, and Sam are here. They are having sex again. It is like working with two pigs in heat. And I don't even get to listen. That is just not fair." Jimmy came out of his office.

Jimmy was the other guy who helped Sam's family. They were both at his mother's funeral and paid for everything. T-Jay was surprised that they knew Sam and had the same last name.

How could Sam ever pay them back for all the money over the years they had given his family? So Sam got right to the point and said, "How can I ever pay you back for all you two have done for my family?"

Jimmy replied, "You don't owe us anything. We are good." Tim whispered something to him.

T-Jay said, "Boss, I need a new sports car. Sam here was looking at our Vicki, he hit my car."

A big smile came across Jimmy's face, and he said, "Go pick yourself out another white sports car on me and take Sam with you. Then come over tonight for supper at the house. You can stay one night, can't you Sam?" Sam agreed, and Tim was laughing so hard he peed his pants.

T-Jay got his new white sports car and then to the store they went to get Sam some nice clothes to wear to the boss' house for supper. Sam said, "I don't have much money with me."

T-Jay replied, "You don't need any money for this, today." Then they went to T-Jay's white apartment to clean up. Sam put his old clothes in the bag his new clothes came in and cleaned himself up in this white room. Then the guys talked as they waited to go for supper at the boss' house. They had already become good friends as different as they were. T-Jay white suit guy and Sam small town guy.

Sam was a little nervous, but T-Jay said, "They don't want the money back, they have money. Vicki will be there, the woman you were watching walk. She likes you, I can tell."

Sam replied, "Most women don't like me. I don't or never will make much money." Sam was sure Vicki would not even look at him, and T-Jay was tall and nice looking, so it was him.

They drove up in a T-Jay's new white sports car and knocked on the door. Jimmy called out, "Come in now. Vicki gets out here and helps Tim with setting the table." Vicki looked at Sam and took his arm. Jimmy was all smiles. Jimmy said, "Sam, this is Vicki and Vicki this is Sam." Jimmy got up and put his kids in their chairs then he went into the kitchen to help Margo. Margo was the prettiest woman Sam, had ever seen but he knew Margo was the kind of woman a man would kill for and Jimmy was just the man to do that. And Sam had Vicki on his arm. They sat down to eat, and Jimmy said the prayer. Jimmy dished his kids their food then Tim started dishing up food for himself which was a clue we can eat now.

Tim asked Sam a few questions about how his family was doing after their mother's death. Everyone was sorry to hear about this. Margo said, "We have had too many funerals, I just can't go anymore." Jimmy hugged her. Tim put his finger to his throat as if he wanted to throw up.

Then Tim asked, "What is for dessert?" He looked around to make sure there was enough.

Margo replied, "Cherry pie with vanilla ice cream and yes Tim, there is more than one pie."

Tim replied, "I bet it is all cherry pie, Jimmy's favorite. We always have Jimmy's favorite and never mind." The kids were laughing, and so was Margo, but Jimmy said nothing while they ate.

After eating, Jimmy said, "Vicki, take Sam out to see the gardens. I have to put the kids to sleep and then I want to talk to Sam." So Vicki took Sam's arm, and they went out to the gardens. She was the only woman who ever understood Sam. They talked about all Sam's ideas and dreams. Sam almost forgot about the talk with Jimmy. Sarah had brought T-Jay another book to read to her, and she sat by him. Linda was busy clearing Tim up from eating.

After Margo and Jimmy put the twins to bed, it was Sarah's turn, but she said to T-Jay before she went off to bed, "Remember my birthday is next week and you just have to come." Jimmy and Margo laughed then Margo gave T-Jay a birthday invite from little Sarah as Jimmy took her to bed.

T-Jay went out to get Sam and Vicki for Jimmy would be ready to talk to Sam. No one kept Jimmy waiting. Vicki kissed Sam on the lips, and he was in heaven. But then T-Jay said, "Go to the library to talk with Jimmy." Sam was scared, and T-Jay added, "I'll just wait here for you."

Jimmy said to Sam, "Sit down a minute. I don't want any money back for anything, but I could use a little help over Sarah's birthday with security. I am putting in a new program for security here at the house if you could stay to help me? It will just take a few days."

Sam smiled and agreed. Then Sam went with T-Jay and stayed at his apartment for what was to be only a few days. But from that day on, Sam never left and never worked anywhere else. Sam, started dating Vicki, and then he wanted to marry Vicki. Vicki wanted Sam to have a good paying job, and Jimmy did pay very nicely. Vicki's parents agreed to let Sam marry their daughter when Sam told them he would be working for Jimmy. Margo helped Sam get a big diamond for Vicki and Jimmy would take the cost out of Sam's paycheck forever. Sam's first date with Vicki was to Sarah's birthday party with someone called Marci who Margo liked very much, and Marci got to talk with Jimmy. She was even seen alone with Jimmy. What was up with this?

Sam didn't care, he took Vicki to eat at a very nice café and asked her to marry him. Vicki said, Yes, and the wedding was on before Sam knew what hit him. Sam called his sister and told her, but all she did was laugh. But T-Jay wanted a wife too, and Jimmy told Sam to go with T-Jay to find him the girl of his dreams. Sam was not sure how to do that, but T-Jay was his best friend. How hard could that be? So Sam, like T-Jay, always said yes to anything Jimmy wanted.

Vicki and her mother were busy planning the wedding, so Sam and T-Jay set out on a Saturday morning to find the woman for T-Jay. T-Jay said, "We'll start in the hills, I want a girl like Heidi."

Sam started thinking, "I am in a white sports car with a guy in a white suit driving around on the countryside looking for Heidi in hills?" Not good, but what could Sam do?

But then as it always does, things got worse. The car overheated and stopped in an old run-down farm. T-Jay got out of the car and followed a blonde girl in cutoffs and t-shirt. Sam would have gotten out too, but her father had a shotgun in his nose. Sam said, "We need a little water for the car has overheated."

The man said, "Twenty dollars for the water." Sam handed the man twenty dollars and looked for a pail. Then the man said, "Twenty more dollars if you need a pail for the water." Sam handed the man another twenty dollars. The car was good again but where was T-Jay? T-Jay would not leave without the girl. Sam knew her father would not let them take his daughter.

Sam said, "T-Jay, let us make a run for it and leave the girl."

T-Jay said, "No, I am not leaving this girl. I want her. Let us run to the barn or her father will shoot us." So to the barn, they run with the farmer's daughter. The farmer started shooting at the barn where they were, so the daughter, named Sally, showed them a back way out of the barn. But T-Jay would not leave the girl, so they run with her to the closest town, and Sam called Jimmy for help. Jimmy was on his way, and the father was in that town looking for them.

Sam heard Jimmy's voice, and he was talking to someone, but who? Then Sam looked and saw it was the girl's father. Jimmy said, "Boys, come out here, now!" Sam and T-Jay with the girl got up and went to Jimmy. Jimmy was mad and asked, "Did you take this man's daughter? Give her back to him. What were you two thinking?" Sam looked at T-Jay and was wondering what?

T-Jay answered Jimmy, "No thinking at all here, sir." Then the man took his daughter to his old truck and put her inside. Jimmy went to talk to the man again. Jimmy came back.

Jimmy said, "Boys, you have to make this good with Mr. Jones on taking his daughter. You have to clean out the pig barns. Now, so get in the back of his truck, and we will follow you there."

T-Jay was all pleased, but Sam was just not sure, so he whispered to Jimmy, "I called you to help us and how is this helping?"

Jimmy replied, "My understanding of the issue is that T-Jay wants that girl and he is still with her. So clean out that pig barn." Jimmy got on back into the limo, the guys got on the back of the truck on an old road with dust. The pig barn was so bad, as the man gave them shovels. T-Jay's white suit was not white anymore. Hours it took, and Jimmy had lunch with the man and his wife with Margo, Tim laughing having fun as they worked. The girl, Sally, brought out cold water for them to drink and her mother looked T-Jay over closely. Then Jimmy said, "Margo, ride in the front with the driver, these guys smell bad. You guys have to go out there a few more times to clean the other pig barns until you have made it up to Mr. and Mrs. Jones with their only child, Sally." Sam wanted to hit something, but T-Jay was happy.

When they got back, Tim said, "Hey guys, here is Mickey, a new guy who will be working with you. He doesn't talk much, but he is very smart with computers. We need him, be nice."

Sam Elgin, T-Jay Pederson, and Mickey Johnson were now the guys working with Jimmy. Merit and Mark were more Margo's guys, and they watched Jimmy very closely. Was it for protection or was Margo just very jealous? Tim was equal to Jimmy and Margo. So Sam, T-Jay, and Mickey had to completely clean out all the barns on Sally's dad's farm. Then T-Jay wanted to marry Sally, so Jimmy talked to her father, Karl Jones. They made a deal if T-Jay could give Karl a grandson after he married his daughter, Sally, then her dad would not kill T-Jay. Sam didn't think that was a good idea, but Jimmy did. T-Jay agreed but brought Karl a new four-wheel drive truck which the old man did like, and Sally's mom was just so nice, like Sally.

They were eating breakfast at Jimmy's house, and he had made french toast for his children with the guys eating too. When Jimmy took a bite of his french toast, T-Jay, Sam, Mickey, and even Tim took a bite of their french toast. Sarah was watching and laughing with the twin over this, but Jimmy looked annoyed. Then Mickey said, "I want one too." Tim was so pleased Mickey was talking more but what did he mean? What did Mickey want too?

Jimmy pointed to the library for Sam and T-Jay to come to talk with him after breakfast. So they did, but they were afraid Jimmy was very moody. T-Jay whispered to Sam. "I heard Jimmy gets very moody the months of June and July. The employees gossip a lot about their bosses in the bathrooms. Just listen sometime." Sam nodded okay.

In the library, Jimmy said, "T-Jay and Sam, tomorrow is Saturday. Take Mickey with you and find him a woman. Mickey wants a wife too." Sam just looked at T-Jay like what the hell?

T-Jay replied to Jimmy, "Yes sir, Sam and I are on it. Don't worry, we got this." And out the door, T-Jay went with Sam following him. Jimmy went to work with Tim and Mickey. Margo came later with Merit and Mark.

Sam said, "T-Jay, are you crazy? How are we going to find Mickey a wife?"

T-Jay replied, "We will take Mickey with us and drive around for awhile then come back. In church later we should find a girl to marry Mickey. He is not a bad guy and will make a lot of money working for Jimmy. Tim is his trainer." Sam agreed that was a good plan and he didn't want to ever say no to Jimmy. What could go wrong?

T-Jay and Sam got Mickey and were driving around just anywhere talking about their life with upcoming weddings. Sam said, "T-Jay, you and Sally are a little different. Have you noticed? Sally wears cut offs and T-shirts with no shoes. You wear white suits with white shoes."

T-Jay replied, "No, I didn't notice any difference between Sally and me. But what about Vicki and you? Vicki buys her clothes in Paris, France and you get anything off the rake at Wal-Mart. Is that going to be a problem for you? I say no, love is just that, its love, no one knows why."

Sam agreed, and they drove on talking, stopping to get snacks and use the restrooms. Then Sam noticed Mickey was not in the back seat. Sam said, "T-Jay, where is Mickey?" T-Jay looked back.

T-Jay said, "What the hell, we lost Mickey? We better go back to every place we stopped and look for him. Jimmy will be very mad about us losing Mickey." And they looked but no Mickey.

Sam said, "This time you call Jimmy. I called him last time with Sally's dad trying to kill us." T-Jay agreed and called Jimmy. Then T-Jay just sat down looking sick. Sam asked, "Was Jimmy mad? What did he say? Will he help us find Mickey?"

T-Jay replied, "Oh yes, Jimmy was mad. He is on is way here. Maybe he will kill us."

Sam answered, "We should maybe run for it before Jimmy gets here."

T-Jay replied, "No, they have our women. Sally's dad doesn't like me, and without Jimmy, I don't think he will let me marry her. And Vicki's parents I am sure will not let you marry her without you working for Jimmy and making a lot of money. So they have our women, and I am not leaving without Sally." Sam agreed, he couldn't leave without Vicki, so they waited.

Jimmy came with Tim and slammed the car door as he got out. Tim even looked mad. Jimmy said, "You two go back and check again on all the places you stopped. Ask people if they saw Mickey? Here is a picture of him." Tim handed Sam the picture of Mickey, and they left. Sam and T-Jay did what Jimmy told them to, but they had no luck at all. Then they drove back to the place they had waited for Jimmy. They just sat there not saying a word to each other. Jimmy drove up alone with the driver. Where was Tim? Jimmy got out and said, "We found Mickey, follow me." They went to an old building where no one had lived for a long time, it was very run down with no lights, and it was dark now. They had all missed Saturday night church. In the building, they followed Jimmy to a floor where Tim sat on the floor with Mickey, a woman, and two kids. They were eating food out of cans. Jimmy said, "Tim you are sure you want to stay the night with Mickey, and his new girlfriend with her brother and sister?"

Tim replied, "Yes, I am okay here, if Mickey is here, then I am. Mickey will not leave this girl, and she will not take her brother and sister with us. She is afraid. She thought Mickey was homeless like they are because she was eating out of the garbage and Mickey ate with them."

Sam and T-Jay had never seen a homeless person before, just on TV, but this was completely different and too sad. Jimmy said, "We will go home and be back in the morning. Margo may have an idea of what to do for Mickey with this girl with her brother and sister. It is warm outside so you should be okay, but I will leave the limo just in case with the driver. T-Jay and Sam, I will ride home with you guys." And they left. Jimmy didn't say a word all the way home and just went into his house. Sam and T-Jay went to T-Jay's apartment until morning. Then they all went to church with the kids and after church out to get Tim, Mickey and the girl with the kids.

Jimmy stopped to get food at a fast food place, and Margo was writing something down. Vicki was still at her parents, planning their wedding and Sally was with her parents at the farm. When they got there, Margo went to talk to the girl as Jimmy gave food out for his kids with the girl's brother and sister. Then they all sat on the floor and ate. Jimmy and Tim acted like it was no big deal. Margo and the girl named Virginia came and ate too, sitting on the floor. Margo had convinced Virginia to come back with them and work for her to help with the children. Margo would have Virginia, her brother Lee and sister Kelly to come with them and living with them to work. Jimmy was very pleased with this, and his kids loved to play with Lee and Kelly

Jimmy whisper to T-Jay and Sam, "Help bring their things, but remember these things are all they have, so be careful with them. Show some respect. Oh, Sam, Vicki needs to stay with her parents until you are married because we will have Virginia and those kids in the house now." Sam was not sure about this because Jimmy and Margo had a very big house, so there's room. They all left in the limo and Lee, and Kelly loved the limo. Margo talked a lot with Virginia about the work she needed her to do for them. Mickey was pleased he had his woman. Jimmy whispered to Mickey, "Go slow with her or you may lose her. Start by being friends then date."

Things looked good, and everything was working out. Then Margo said one Sunday after church to the guys, "Jimmy and I want to give you guys a wedding gift of a house built the way you want it for a price and new furniture for a shower gift." Jimmy made a sound. Tim laughed.

Sam said, "They don't have to do that for us." T-Jay agreed.

Tim replied, "Oh don't worry about the cost for Jimmy. He will get some great sex for this."

Margo started with the building of their homes, Vicki's was a modern home, and Sally's home was a ranch style house. Margo had the houses built close to them and a space left for Mickey's one. The houses were completed and the weddings planned for late August and September. T-Jay's was in late August and was out at Sally's family farm. It was a picnic, and T-Jay's parents wore black. T-Jay had a white suit on, and Sally had a white dress with no shoes. Everyone had a great time, and Jimmy with Tim sang a song for everyone to dance to after the pastor married them and they ate hot dogs, beer, potato salads and pie for a wedding cake.

Sam and Vicki's wedding was in September, and it was very formal. They ate food Sam didn't know what it was and drank wine. The cake was tall and all colors. Everyone had a nameplate on where to sit to eat. Tim and Jimmy sang songs and everyone danced. The pastor did the wedding in a formal church service. Sam was happy, and his sister came with her husband.

The twins' birthday came and Halloween which Sam with T-Jay had to work to protect Jimmy as he took his kids trick or treating. It was good they had Virginia's brother and sister to go too.

At Thanksgiving, Margo gave them different times to come so Tim could have three big meals to eat. Linda got the paper on orders of what not to say. Never say the word FREEZER or ask, what are the sins of the family that I don't know? The guys were not sure of this, but okay.

Christmas Eve was private and then church but Christmas day they could all come over to Jimmy's home, Margo told them. So T-Jay and Sam planned to be with their wives' family for Christmas Eve then leave in time to go to church with Jimmy's family. Mickey planned to ask Virginia to marry him on Christmas Eve then dinner out with gifts for her brother and sister and church. Things did not go as planned. Mickey got down on one knee and said, "Well you marry me?" And he showed Virginia a very nice diamond ring. But Virginia grabbed her brother and sister then ran to the bus station. Mickey ran after her and Tim ran after Mickey. Jimmy didn't look happy, and Margo motioned him to go and help. At the bus station, Virginia and kids were on the bus to go somewhere. Mickey laid down in front of the bus so it could not leave. Tim was out of breath, but Mickey had stopped breathing.

Tim cried, "Jimmy, give Mickey mouth to mouth, or he will die."

Jimmy got out of the limo and said, "I like Mickey but if I have to give him mouth to mouth or he will die. Then he is just going to have to die for I am not doing that." Virginia ran out of the bus and gave Mickey mouth to mouth so he would start breathing again, and thankfully, it worked.

Tim said, "Virginia, Mickey will die without you."

Virginia said, "I am not good enough for Mickey."

Jimmy said, "Then Mickey will have to die." So Virginia came home with Mickey and took his ring to marry him. The kids were happy, and Mickey did not die that day. Tim was a little mad at Jimmy, but it all worked out. T-Jay and Sally and Vicki and Sam are all expecting babies to be born soon.

Christmas day went good, and all heard about the event. Mickey and Virginia were married on a cold January day as soon as possible. Mickey was very happy. Margo had a house built with furniture for them too, and Jimmy made his grunting sound again, but all was good. T-Jay lived on the right side of Jimmy's home, Sam in the back, and Mickey on the left, the front had the driveways with gardens. All was secure.

T-Jay and Sally's baby was born, and it was a boy. Sally's dad named the baby C-Jay Karl Jones Pederson. Sam was working on a new security system at Jimmy's house again, an upgrade.

Vicki called Sam saying, "My water broke."

Sam replied, "Call the plumber, the number is on the desk." Vicki called Sam all kinds of the name so Sam called Jimmy to complain, "She should just call the plumber."

Jimmy said, "What?" Jimmy was in his moody time again, but Sam was not getting it. Jimmy continued, "Go home and get your wife to the hospital! Tim and I will meet you there. Your baby is coming out now." Sam drove home and took Vicki to the hospital as Jimmy told him.

Vicki cried, "Does Jimmy have to tell you everything? It is a surprise I got pregnant without you asking him how or did you?" Tim motioned not to answer her and stand away from being hit.

Sam's baby boy was born, and all was forgotten. Sam and Vicki named the baby Samuel Alan Elgin. Sam brought his wife and son home with joy, but then things didn't go right from the start. Sam asked Vicki, "Do you think Samuel wants pancakes for breakfast?" Vicki threw a bottle of milk at him, so he called Jimmy to complain that Vicki was not nice to him.

Jimmy replied, "Let the white-haired people in your house feed the baby." Then Jimmy hung up the phone is Sam's ear.

Sam saw something gold come out of his son's head and then the boy just disappeared. Sam ran to Jimmy for help and told Jimmy all about it. Jimmy said nothing.

Tim said, "Sam, your wife is from another planet, and she is an alien. Jimmy is from the same planet. They have antennas, they can disappear then reappear at will, and they can read minds. Jimmy's antennas are silver for he is the leader and all the others are gold antennas. Jimmy needs to have a baby girl with silver antennas to rule the people on this other planet."

Sam sat down on the chair. Was he having a nervous breakdown? Shouldn't a woman tell you first if they are from another planet before you marry them and have a child?

Jimmy said, "Tim, stop it. Sam take a few days off and talk with Vicki's parents then I will answer any questions you have. Get some rest. We will help you with your son, don't worry." Sam did just that, and he never asked any more questions about it again. Sam went for drives.

T-Jay was okay, but then T-Jay had his father-in-law to take care of his son. Sally's dad was over every day after T-Jay went to work and stayed there most of the day. Sally's mom was also at T-Jay's home a lot, but T-Jay was okay with that because they helped with the baby. Sally's parents even took the baby with them for weekends, so T-Jay had alone time with Sally.

Mickey decided not ever to have any children. They had his wife's brother and sister to raise. Mickey was not taking any chances in this. Sam looked stressed.

Sam did go for long drives by himself and one time he saw a girl crying by the side of the road, and he stopped. The girl told Sam her family needs food so Sam went to her family and gave them money to start a business so they could make money, then Sam went home but told no one. Sam remembered how Jimmy and Tim helped his family and never told anyone or asked for the money back, so he tried to do the same.

A week later, Sam came home and Vicki threw a pot at Sam, so he called Jimmy.

Sam said, "Jimmy, I think Vicki is trying to cook, but she doesn't know how because she throws a pot at me. Could Margo teach Vicki how to cook?"

Jimmy said, "Sam, my boy, if she throws a pot at your head she thinks you are seeing another woman. Are you?"

Sam replied, "No, I did give some girl some money for her family to start a business so they could make money to buy food. Like you and Tim helped my family, remember? Tell no one but God's knows the good you do."

Jimmy said, "Sam, oh Sam. When we gave your family that money I told my wife, Margo, first and asked if that would be okay with her. Never give another woman money without first asking your wife if you should. Or you will not have a wife very long." Sam started to cry.

Then on the table, Sam saw a thank you note from the girl and her family for the money he gave them for the business. Vicki was thinking the worst. Had Sam done nothing wrong, had he? Jimmy came over and first talked to Vicki to find out how mad she was, and it was bad. Then Jimmy sat Sam down and said, "You make too much money to get divorced, and you have a kid. Never give any other women any money without Vicki okaying it first. Now to get you out of this mess. Buy Vicki something that she wants that cost about the same as the money you gave that girl's family. Tell Vicki the truth that you are that dumb and you did not see it as she sees it. Let Vicki know that she is right and you are an idiot. Then let her talk and agree with anything she says. Got it." Then Jimmy just left.

Sam cried, but he did what Jimmy told him to, and Vicki was not mad anymore. Vicki wanted a new car and another baby. So Sam got Vicki any car she wanted, and they went right to work on making the new baby.

Tim was smiling at Sam. T-Jay and Mickey just looked down. Did anyone believe Sam that he had done nothing with this girl but try to help her family?

Jimmy said, "Sometimes we don't know how good we have it until we almost lose it. Think boys before you do something dumb. Just think first, how will your wife react to what you have done? I am not a damn marriage counselor." But as Jimmy said those words he was sure he would be eating them soon, but why? Because he was a guy too and he knew he could mess up at any given time and be just where Sam was. Jimmy also worried about having a wife fifteen years younger than him. Would she want someone closer to her age someday soon? Would she break his heart to love another man? Jimmy also knew he was still in love with Sylvia.

CHAPTER FIVE

VIDEO TAPES, THE TRUTH AND MORE

Tim came out running, and Mickey ran up to him saying, "What happened? Are you okay? Where is Jimmy?" Tim sat down to breathe and pointed to a room that was locked. Jimmy had just gotten it opened and went in. T-Jay, Sam, and Mickey walked in slowly to find Jimmy, and he was there with walls and walls of videotapes. Mickey asked, "What's on the tapes? Do you want us to fix them up so we can see them? I can do that for you."

Jimmy replied, "Yes. But be careful with them. I want to study them. Tim is working on a history thing for the past of the guys we knew before you guys came. There may be unbelievable things to see. The truth is on these tapes."

Tim said, "Now boys, let's tell no one about them until we know more. Keep this door locked. Just the five of us should know for now. Not even Margo, okay Jimmy?" Jimmy agreed which surprised the guys, this was new. They started the work just a few hours a day, but it turned out to be very interesting. Someone named Larry had videoed people without them knowing it. Tim and Jimmy looked so young on the tapes. It took a few months, but the tapes were ready for viewing. Jimmy could hardly wait, and this was not like him. T-Jay, Sam, and Mickey whispered to each other what was up with Jimmy? Tim appeared to know but was not telling anyone, anything about it.

The video starts at Mr. King's house, and Tim's mother is there collecting clothes for a church, but they can't see the name on the bags. Then she walks down a long hallway to the door. Just then Karen, Jim's wife comes to the window with a gun and shoots toward Mrs. King which hits her in the head. One shot and she is down on the floor. But did Tim's mom hear the shot? Karen crawls under Tim's mom's car, but why?

No, Mickey makes it bigger to see, and Karen is cutting the brake line. Then Karen just rolling into the trees just before Tim's mom drives off in the car. Karen runs down the back-way home. The road to Mr. King's house is windy, and the hills are steep. Tim's mom tries the brakes, but they do not work, and off the road, she goes down the hill as the car rolls. The guys see where Larry had to have the camera up to see this shot and video it. The camera is working and it's not just cheap equipment. Bob was doing the videoing, and they got a good look at him doing it. But why did Larry want this?

Tim got up and walked around. Jimmy asked, "Do you want to take a break?" Tim shook his head no, so they continued. There was no movement in the car and hours later a workman found her. He goes for help, but the police cars are blocking the road taking Mrs. King out.

The video continues at Jim and John's café where Anna works where a police officer enters the cafe to talk with Anna. They can't hear what is said, but Anna starts to cry. Jim has her sit down, then the officer leaves. Jim says, "Anna, I know how to get where your mom is fast, let's go." John nods okay, and Jim with Anna go up the hill in the back of the Cafe by foot. They take a shortcut through the woods to find Tim's mom right away. She is still alive and talks to Anna but what she tells Anna is something they couldn't hear. That meant the guys who are taping this never got it. The ambulance comes with Tim and Joey. To the hospital, they all go with Tim's mom in the ambulance. In the ambulance, Joey tries to talk to his mom, but she does not answer him. So Larry had a video camera in the ambulance. Tim's father is at the hospital, but his mom has already died. There is a lot of people walking around crying. Mrs. King is dead.

There is some video of the two funerals but not much. Mrs. King's was a very big costly funeral, and Tim's mom's was less expensive. About the same people are at both, only more for Mrs. King. They see Mr. King with his son and daughter crying. Tim's dad and the boys with Anna are crying too at Tim's mom's funeral. Tim just closes his eyes. Jimmy says, "Boys, this is enough for today. Let us start tomorrow at noon. It means a lot to Tim and me, thanks."

The next day, they all sat down to see the next video, and it was Anna kissing Jim behind the café in the alley. Jim says "I love you, and I am telling Karen today that we are over. I will meet you tonight at your place at 10 PM." Then they kiss again, and Anna starts to leave. Jim asks, "Will you marry me?" Jim gives Anna a ring that she takes, and Tim looks at Jimmy.

Tim said, "I never even knew Anna was in love with Jim. He never told me, but why?"

Jimmy replied, "Maybe we will see it all." Mickey looks at Jimmy, and he nodded to continue the video where they see Jim goes to talk with Karen.

Jim says to Karen, "We are through. I love another. Please understand and set me free."

Karen looks mad saying, "When hell freezes over. I am knocked up, and it is yours. Gerald tells me it is twins. You will marry me, or I will tell Larry, and his new Daddy, Mr. King that you got me pregnant and now will not man up to it and marry me."

Jim looks sad but goes to Gerald who does show him papers of some kind. Then Jim cries. At about 5 AM Jim goes to Anna's place and there he sees a lot of people. Jim tries to make his way through the crowd and sees Anna on the floor shot in the head. Jim falls to the ground and cries. Charles comes and picks him up and takes Jim to the hospital. The video is on Jim. Larry's mom has her wedding that night to Mr. King, and all the police and important people were at the wedding, so it was not clear when Anna got shot. But Tim remembers it was just starting to become daylight when he heard the shot. Tim cries here, and Jimmy with Mickey help him. After Tim settles down, they watch the videotape over and over again. Tim wanted to see his mom and Anna one more time alive. Jimmy tells Mickey to let Tim see it as many times as he wants. Mickey agrees to do that for Tim as Sam and T-Jay sit there watching it all.

The next tape was of Jimmy in a church with a thin blonde haired girl who bounced all over when she walked. Jimmy was following her all over the place. They were reading the Bible together and talked about it. Then they were teaching little children about God. Going to church on Sunday and looking at each other. But it looked like the girl's parents didn't like Jimmy. Jimmy was always looking at the girl, and Tim said, "That is Sylvia, Jimmy's first love." Jimmy did not take his eyes off the video. After that, each day Jimmy would watch the short video of Sylvia. Margo noticed the change in Jimmy and was asking what was going on at work?

Tim made everyone promise not to tell Margo because he was sure she would not take it well, Jimmy watching his first love over and over again. Jimmy could not stop, it was like he was in love with Sylvia all over again. Jimmy started coming early to work, right after breakfast with his kids. Jimmy also came at night to watch and see his Sylvia. Tim tried to talk with Jimmy on this, about Margo finding out but Jimmy couldn't stop himself. He just had to see Sylvia more and more. What would happen if Margo found out? Tim reminded the guys, "Sylvia is dead, and Jimmy can't cheat on Margo with a dead girl. So continue the work." Mickey did, and he put one more video together for Jimmy and Tim to watch. But at home, Margo was asking Jimmy all kinds of questions, and he was saying nothing. Tim tried to stop Margo, but the questioning went on day and night. Margo even came to work to ask Jimmy what was going on but he said, "Nothing." Margo was looking everywhere. Merit and Mark were helping her, but Tim told no one, not even Linda. The guys didn't even tell their wives. Jimmy had to stop watching the video so Margo wouldn't find them. Mickey made Jimmy a picture of Sylvia from the videotapes made by Bob and Larry. Jimmy just loved the picture. The guys made a secret room for the videotapes where Mickey could work on them alone with only Tim's help.

The new videotape Mickey found was the killer; it was about the car accident Jimmy and Silvia were in before Sylvia disappeared. It had been in pieces, but why? Did someone just cut it up? They sat down to watch it. The tape starts with Jimmy and Sylvia coming out of nowhere to Jimmy's car. It was after Tim had just driven the car home. Tim went inside the house with his son, Merit. Jimmy and Sylvia didn't go into the house. Jimmy put a wedding dress in the trunk of the car. Then they drove away, and on the railroad, the car just stops. There was a train coming very fast. Jimmy got out of the car and got Sylvia out of the car. Jimmy went for the wedding dress in the trunk of the car. Sylvia went running back to the car to get something, and the train hit the car. Jimmy flies back and so does Sylvia. Jimmy ran to find Sylvia; he looked everywhere until he found her. Sylvia says to Jimmy as he holds her close to him, "I feel so cold." Jimmy kissed her lips. Jimmy curled up next to Sylvia and waited for help because he heard the sound of an ambulance. When the ambulance came, they gave Jimmy a shot and took Sylvia away. Then it shows Tim running to Jimmy and the second ambulance came to take Jimmy to the hospital. Everyone was shocked, but Jimmy was crying for his Sylvia.

Tim said, "We will start another day watching the videos. Maybe, Jimmy, we can learn what happened to Sylvia. We can find answers to what happened to Sylvia. It will take time and a lot of work, but Jimmy has done a lot for you guys. I think Sylvia died, but it would be nice to know when and how. Jimmy needs closure on this to move forward with Margo now." Then Tim took Jimmy home, he was shaking all over and very upset.

Margo was all over Tim asking what was going on with Jimmy. Tim answered, "Jimmy is sick of all your questioning. So stop it, now." But at work, Margo started flirting with guys. Tim tried to stop her before Jimmy noticed. But Jimmy's mind was on Sylvia and how to get away from Margo to see the videos. Margo was acting out to get Jimmy's attention, but he was too into the videos and seeing Sylvia just one more time. Margo was sure that Jimmy was cheating on her with some other woman.

Tim answered Margo by saying, "No, Jimmy is not cheating on you with another woman. I would know. Don't you trust me?" Margo settled down after that and Jimmy was happier. Sam was to complete another new security system for Jimmy's house, so he went without calling first. Sam was sure he saw Margo at work with Jimmy. But when Sam got there, there was no one home, not even the white-hair people. So Sam used his key and went inside. He started to work. Then he heard a sound from the bedroom of Margo and Jimmy. Sam went to look and found Margo in bed with another man.

The guy just ran out the window, and Margo put on clothes and cried to Sam, "Please don't tell Jimmy. He would be so hurt. I love Jimmy, but I made a mistake, I had never been with another man but Jimmy so I just wanted to know how it would be. I will never do it again. Please don't tell him." Margo was on her knees.

So Sam agreed, but he said, "If Jimmy finds out he will kill me. So never again, okay? Was it worth it? Was he any better than Jimmy in bed?"

Margo replied, "No, it was not good at all. I want my Jimmy. What have I done? I hate myself. I am jealous. I thought he is seeing Sylvia, his first love. But she is dead right? Have you heard anything? It makes me crazy thinking about Jimmy and that Sylvia. I can't live without Jimmy. I am a mess, but I will make this up to Jimmy. Just wait and see. I will love him and be so good to him that he will never leave me."

Sam answered, "Jimmy can't cheat on you with a dead girl, and he would never cheat on you," Margo smiled, and they never talked about it again. Margo was nicer to Jimmy.

But he didn't stop watching the videos. Was it to find out how Sylvia died or was it to see her again? There were so many questions like, why did Larry video the accident? Was the shot they gave Jimmy to help him or make him forget about what happened? Why was Sylvia not on the police report after the accident? Did Sylvia's parents take her away somewhere? Did Sylvia die? They needed to watch more of the videos to find out clues to help them. Tim and Jimmy had looked for Sylvia for years, and now they were so close to the answer. They had to know.

CHAPTER SIX

KEVIN CARLSON, THE LAWYER, AND TRUSTED FRIEND

Margo had burned her and Jimmy's bed, but Jimmy said nothing about it. Tim asked about it, but no one answered him. Margo was taking a shower all the time. Sam knew what was up with that. But business continues, and Tim said, "Who knows with women? Let her do whatever. We have a graduation to go to." Tim and Jimmy went out the door, but to where? Sam went to Mickey to see if he knew anything. T-Jay went in Mickey's office who was working on videos.

Sam asked, "Does anyone know about this graduation and why Margo is burning her bed?" Sam wanted to know if anyone else knew what had happened at Margo's home that day.

Mickey replied, "No one understands why women do what they do, not even women. Tim and Jimmy have been paying for Eric's nephews' education since their mother left them and their dad has issues. Tim is hoping the twins will come and work at the company with research law. In other words, to help find this person they want with the little black sports car, not new or expensive, somewhere, this person fits into finding of Sylvia or figuring out what happened."

T-Jay said, "Where did we find the black sports car? I didn't see that one. Who has a black sports car in their past?"

Mickey replied, "I only have pieces of this tape, and I know Jimmy knows who has a black sports car and it is a key to Sylvia. T-Jay, are you okay? You look a little sick. What is up with you? I know you have been to the doctor."

T-Jay answered, "I had myself fixed. I don't want any more children. I don't think the pill is that safe for Sally."

Sam said, "You what? Had yourself fixed like they do a dog?" T-Jay nodded yes. Sam was still on the name Eric and was thinking he was the guy Sam saw jump out of Margo's bedroom window. Sam knew he could not tell the guys this. T-Jay went on to tell them how it didn't hurt at all and how easy it was. Then he looked at Mickey who just shook his head no. Sam said, "Vicki and I are having another baby." The guys smiled and nodded okay. No more was said.

A few days later, Jimmy called a meeting with the guys. T-Jay, Sam, and Mickey walked into Jimmy's office, and there sat three other guys. Tim said, "Sam, T-Jay, and Mickey meet Aaron, Daron, and Kevin. Jimmy thinks we need legal researchers and a lawyer who is Kevin Carlson. Daron and Aaron are Eric Erup's nephews and are here, so let us all get along. Kevin what kind of lawyer, are you? What kind of business law did you study at the university?"

Kevin replied, "I am a divorce lawyer. I am not sure why I am here, but they made me an offer I couldn't say no. The money was that good. But what will I be doing?"

Tim's eyes were the biggest, and no one said a word until Jimmy said, "Tim will train Kevin on the company standards. Aaron, you are marrying your girlfriend, April. Margo will train you and Daron I will train you myself." Daron looked afraid. Jimmy was moody again. Kevin loved working with Tim. No one saw them do any real work, but they had drinks, ate out a lot, and took naps. Aaron took his girlfriend April with him to work with Margo so April could take notes for Aaron. He didn't miss anything about the training. Daron had a lot of work to do with Jimmy. Most of the time, Daron had no idea what Jimmy was telling him, and Jimmy was speaking English. Daron was afraid of Jimmy. Daron went crying to Aaron, and he asked Kevin to help his brother with Jimmy.

Kevin went to Tim. Tim said, "Jimmy is just moody now. He will be over it in two months or so. I can't always understand Jimmy either, and he does speak several languages. Jimmy is a genius and is over our heads in thinking. Tell Daron to hang in there. T-Jay made it through training with Jimmy and liked it." Kevin went back to the twins with this information which didn't help Daron at all. Daron talked about leaving the company, but Aaron felt they owed the company their education and to work for awhile to pay them back. Daron agreed. Kevin knew Aaron just wanted to make money so he could marry April and Kevin liked the money too. Kevin had bought a few new cars. Kevin also was to marry, but he forgot her name. Kevin was sure Jimmy wanted married guys around his pretty wife.

Aaron and April got married, and so Kevin married Alice. Jimmy and Margo gave them a home built the way they wanted it with furniture at an agreed cost. Jimmy did make a sound when Margo told them, but Tim smiled. April and Aaron had a nice wedding with only her parents and his father, a very quiet man who Jimmy with Tim made feel welcome and special. Kevin's wedding was big and very costly. Kevin and Tim danced with all the women, but Kevin's new wife was okay with that because Kevin was making a lot of money doing what, no one knew. Kevin's parents were very proud of him. It had been a bad time for them because Kevin's only older sister's husband had left her with a couple of kids for another woman. Kevin's first divorce case? Kevin asked Jimmy, "Could I help my sister in her divorce while working for you?"

Jimmy answered, "Yes, it will give you some experience which I hope you will never have to use for me." Kevin smiled back but walked away in shock had Jimmy just told him his problems?

After the weddings, Daron was still complaining about Jimmy being impossible at work. His moody time was over, and he was still moody. And Sam's wife had her baby, so Daron got to be with Jimmy more so Sam could take some time off to be with his wife and new baby. Sam, T-Jay, and Mickey didn't like Kevin, Aaron, and Daron, so they were not helpful to them. Daron knew nothing about what he was doing for Jimmy. Aaron knew the security codes, and he was working on finding Tim and Margo's family history.

Kevin didn't have a clue what Tim did but to drink, eat, and nap. Jimmy had told him to keep working with Tim, so he did. Daron had checked with everyone to help him with Jimmy, even T-Jay who they called white suit guy, Sam who they called the boy Scott, and Mickey they called the computer guy with no help from any of them. Daron went to Merit and Mark. They knew nothing about anything, so why were they there? Then Aaron asked Margo to help Daron, and she agreed to go to his office to look at what Jimmy and Daron worked on. Margo was walking into Daron's office, looked at the paperwork, then walked out, and he never saw her again. Margo said nothing to Daron or Aaron or even Kevin about it.

School started, Halloween, twin's birthday, Thanksgiving, Christmas, New Years, Easter, and then Sarah's birthday with Marci. The first time Kevin, Aaron, and Daron saw Marci. It was a different place, and Kevin felt right at home. But Aaron and Daron couldn't wait to leave, and the got their wish. Margo and Marci had a big fight. Jimmy took Margo home because she was so angry and was hitting Marci. Marci didn't hit back. No one said, "catfight" about the two.

Catifight is a word sometimes used when women fight with each other, and guys laugh at it.

Daron said, as they got home, "The other guys got six months of training, and we are only getting three months of training. What's up with that?"

Aaron replied, "So you want more work with Jimmy? I thought you said he was moody as all hell. You had no idea what he was teaching you to do. Now you are complaining it is over?"

Kevin said, "I think my training with Tim continues because Jimmy told me to continue working with Tim. But we haven't done anything even close to working. I like it and want more of it. I have the time to work on my sister's divorce, good practice Jimmy told me."

It was a few days after the catfight on a sunny day when Jimmy was working on something in Daron's office, which Daron had no idea what they were doing. It was like an answer to Daron's prayer; Jimmy got a message to come to Marci. Jimmy left right away to see her. Was this why Margo and Marci had their fight over Jimmy seeing Marci too much alone? Margo was jealous. Daron had not even seen Jimmy leave, but as fast as Jimmy was gone, he was back and called a meeting of the guys. Jimmy said, "Marci is shot, dead. I want us to find who has killed Marci and why? I want the guy, and I want to kill him myself. Understand everyone?" Tim, Merit, Mark, T-Jay, Sam, Mickey, Kevin, Daron, and Aaron were in the meeting only but no Margo, with Jimmy talking. Did he not have her come because of the fight or did she not come?

Tim added by saying as Jimmy left the room, "Jimmy is upset and we can't have our genius upset or where will the money come from to pay all of you? We need to find out who killed Marci as soon as possible, now go to it. I will be with Jimmy in his office. Margo is at home crying."

Was this some attack? Would someone be after Jimmy? Were they all in danger? Kevin was on it to watch Jimmy carefully 24/7. The other guys agreed to watch out for Jimmy and his wife with kids. Again Tim said, "What about me?" Everyone just laughed out loud.

Margo told Sam she was afraid Jimmy would blame her for the killing of Marci because of their fight. Sam did know the first thing Jimmy did was to look at the home security system to see where Margo was when Marci was shot. Margo was at home with the kids, alone, with white-haired people. Jimmy moved on from that because the white-haired people were Marci's people and would never lie to Jimmy and he knew that.

Kevin knew that whoever killed Marci didn't want money because she had diamonds on when they found her. There were important documents on the desk. She died in Jimmy and her office with a top security system, but how was the system was turned off. They knew how to turn it off so no one would hear Marci and them fighting. But Marci had not put up a fight, so she knew her killer. Kevin asked Sam, "Who knows the security system?"

Sam replied, "Jimmy, Margo, Marci, and me. I think Jimmy has a mother where Marci lives who may also know it. Then Jimmy's kids may know. They are like little geniuses."

Kevin was on this, and he told Aaron and Daron it is time to work for our pay. Daron was on it with the work Jimmy and him were doing. Daron said, "It is odd that Margo came in once and looked at these papers then had the fight with Marci." They studied the papers, but it was just on the black sports car someone drove. Kevin went to Tim for answers after Marci's funeral.

At the funeral, Marci's husband George was there with two children, a boy and a girl. Then George left as soon as it was over. Jimmy was fine with George leaving but he trusted no one. The funeral was at the place Marci had died, and Jimmy did talk to older women with white hair.

Kevin asked Tim, "Who is the woman with the white hair? What is this place? Where are we? Could Marci have had a boyfriend? Was it Jimmy? Could Marci's husband have found out?"

Tim said, "Slow down, Kevin, with all the questions. I don't know who the older woman is but think it is Jimmy's mother. This place is hard to explain, and you need to ask Jimmy about it. Yes, Marci could have had a boyfriend, and yes, Jimmy and she did sleep together a lot before she married George for the money, I think. I wanted to check those children to see if they were Jimmy's? But Jimmy would not have it, and Marci just laughed about my request. Let us look at the husband, because nothing of value on Marci or the office is gone. Marci knew her killer. Who would Marci let in the office alone with her?"

Kevin replied, "Let's do the check of children to see if they are Jimmy's kids? I think this has something to do with a child, but I don't know where I am getting this idea." Tim just nodded.

They went about their work and were able to check out Marci's two children, and they were not Jimmy's, but George's kids, so that was the end of that. Jimmy was sure it was a person who lived there or was a white hair person because on the outside cameras there were no cars that came to Marci's place to see her. Whoever killed Marci got there in a flash and then left again. There was an unwritten rule that these people who lived there didn't kill one another for any reason.

A month later, Daron called his brother, Aaron, to meet Kevin and him at Aaron's home that night and not to tell anyone about the meeting. What was up with this but Kevin was not sure Daron had something on Marci's killing. Could Jimmy have done it or Sam? Kevin was not sure Sam didn't know how to get to that place without Jimmy. So Sam couldn't have done it. Jimmy's kids were too little to drive there, and Margo was home all day, the cameras showed. Jimmy's mother? As they waited for Daron to come, Kevin's mind was going crazy with who done it? Then the police came to Aaron's home to tell Aaron that his brother, Daron, was in a car accident. Aaron called Jimmy right away, and with Tim, Jimmy came to get Kevin.

Jimmy said, "Aaron, stay with your wife. We don't know what happened yet. Kevin, come with us and write down your thoughts as we look at the car accident." Tim nodded yes for Kevin to do that.

They got to the car accident, and Jimmy had the police let them look it over first before they even removed Daron's dead body. Daron's car just drove off the road into a big hole. Daron was half ways under the steering wheel. Was he trying to get out? The driver's side was upright, but the passenger side was totaled out. It looked like someone else was driving and then just got out but how? Jimmy appeared to understand how this happened and he looked at Kevin's notes. Kevin wrote that he felt the police thought Daron was killed, but had no evidence. They took pictures, and Tim paid the police to look the other way for a minute or two as Jimmy looked at everything with Kevin. Kevin was not sure why he was there, but he did it.

The funeral for Daron was sad, and his father came. Jimmy and Tim put the father up front with Aaron and April. Sam appears to be more upset than the other guys, but why? Sam also didn't like Erik, Daron's uncle. Jimmy even notice it. Tim said to Kevin, "What's up with Sam?"

Jimmy said to the father of Daron and Aaron, "We will get this guy, who killed your son."

Kevin and Aaron started looking through Daron's work. There was something he wanted to tell them and only them, but what? Was Daron afraid of Jimmy or Tim or maybe Sam? Kevin said, "Daron was working on who killed Marci so whoever killed Marci may have killed Daron. Was the paperwork all about the black sports car and a guy named Billy Joe. Who was Billy Joe?"

Kevin went to Tim and asked, "Who is Billy Joe? Who drove a black sports car in your past?"

Tim replied, "I don't know anyone named Billy Joe. Check the high school yearbooks in this area for that name for about all years for the last thirty. But Jimmy had a girlfriend who was married and drove a black sports car. She died in childbirth with his second son, Travis."

Kevin and Aaron did start checking the high school yearbooks, and Kevin got the car's license off of a picture which they blew up. He checked the license plates to see who owned that car at the time of Jimmy's son's death. Then Kevin went to Jimmy with this and asked, "Where are your old girlfriend and her husband? Where can I find them to ask if they know a Billy Joe?"

Jimmy looked at Kevin and said nothing at first, then he replied, "Leave it alone. She never knew a Billy Joe. She died in childbirth with our son, Travis. He came too soon."

Kevin replied, "No, she didn't die in childbirth. She was very sick, and they put her in another hospital. She has a husband and daughter." Jimmy's eyes just lighted up, and a big smile was on his face. It was Kevin who told Jimmy his Sylvia was still alive.

Jimmy said, "Find them for me and tell no one. Daron was working on finding the daughter for me. I had heard the doctor saying she died but then they must have gotten her to breathe again as I took my dead son's body away." Kevin had so many questions to ask Jimmy, but Tim walked into the room, and all talking on Jimmy's part stopped.

After that, Jimmy and Margo were fighting again, but over what, Kevin and Aaron were not sure. The guys, T-Jay, Sam, and Mickey, said it was over Jimmy's dead girlfriend, Sylvia. Was this the same woman who died in childbirth? They said no, she died in a car accident. Kevin went to Tim on this and Tim said, "Jimmy had two dead sons and two dead girlfriends. One dead son was with Venus, and the other was with this married woman who drove the black sports car. Sylvia was the first dead girlfriend, and the married woman was the second one. Kevin knew the married woman was still alive and Jimmy wanted to find her. Had Margo known? Kevin asked one more question to Tim, "Were you sure the baby with the married woman was Jimmy's son?"

Tim replied, "Yes, because the married woman's husband couldn't have children. I am sure because I too looked at the report on him." Kevin was now sure that the married woman also had Jimmy's child named Teresa and the son Travis were both Jimmy's children. Jimmy was not married to Margo at that time. Margo was only in her teens. Could the married woman be Sylvia? Kevin looked at that car accident report. If Sylvia died in the car accident, then there would be a report. Kevin went to Tim again. Tim then told Kevin about the videotapes and told the guys to let Kevin watch them but only Kevin. Kevin was sure Sylvia was still alive but how to prove it? Kevin wrote Jimmy a note on it. Kevin did want to see Marci's whip. He was sure it had nothing to do with her death, but he had to see. Kevin and Jimmy worked on finding Sylvia and Teresa. But they told no one, not even Tim. Margo and Jimmy were fighting a lot, and no one knew why.

Jimmy was at work, and then Tim called Kevin one night after work saying, "Get over here and now." Kevin left right away and walked into Jimmy's house, seeing Jimmy holding his daughter, Tammy about a few years old, and she died. The other two kids were crying and told a sad story of how Tammy found her mommy, Margo in bed with another man and was going to tell her daddy, Jimmy. So the man named Eric hit Tammy and she fell, hitting her head. Michael tried to stop Eric, but Sarah took him away and called for Tammy to get away from Eric so he could not hit her. She didn't make it in time.

One hit to a small child, and she was dead. Jimmy was crying too as he was holding his daughter, Tammy. Sam was there now, with Eric, off to the police and jail for the killing of Tammy. Margo was crying, and Jimmy looked up at Kevin saying, "Have Margo taken to rehab and find out why she didn't stop him from killing our daughter, Tammy. I want a divorce from Margo and now. I want my children and everything else. Do it, Kevin." So Kevin did what Jimmy wanted.

The trial for Eric went fast, and Kevin was going for the death penalty which, he got. Then the divorce, in which Margo didn't want anything and agreed with anything Jimmy wanted, was easy. Everything else was on hold. Aaron continued to work on who killed his brother. Jimmy lived in the house with his children, Sarah and Michael. The funeral was too sad. Margo was not to come, and Kevin made that court order. Margo agreed to stay away; she said she was drunk with drugs which Tim agreed was in her system. Margo would go and live with Merit. Mark, and her mother, Sue, in their old house after rehab.

Eric had been beaten each night in his jail cell even with the guards watching his cell all night. Tim said, "I think he is doing it to himself, or how is that happening?" So, Eric was almost half dead when he got to the gas chamber. Jimmy, Tim, and Kevin came to watch. Margo was taken from the rehab so she could watch Eric die too by Jimmy's request, and Kevin made that happen too. Margo could not sit with Jimmy, so she sat alone. Tim wouldn't talk to her.

Michael's birthday at Tammy's gravesite was sad and he was crying. Michael and Sarah were hugging. For Thanksgiving, Jimmy had Sarah and Michael meet Margo to eat at a café. He waited in the car with Kevin as Tim went in with the kids to eat. Jimmy ate nothing. Tim got Kevin food.

For Christmas, Margo was out of rehab and went to clean the church in clothes no one would recognize her in. Margo cried, cleaning that church for days. Kevin did tell Jimmy what she was doing.

Aaron did look at Eric's statement that he didn't mean to kill the child, that he was high and drunk. But that was no excuse for killing a child. Aaron couldn't believe that he was going to die for his crime. Everyone at the company now hated Aaron too because of what his uncle did.

Work continued at the company and Jimmy work from his home so he could be with Sarah and Michael. Tim ran back and forth with anything Jimmy wanted. For Christmas, Jimmy went to church with his kids. Margo was not to go when Jimmy or the kids were there. Kevin took that order from the courts to Margo, she agreed. Margo had Kevin give gifts to Jimmy and the kids with cards. Margo wrote a note to Jimmy, saying, I am so sorry and understand you can't forgive me.

Merit and Mark just let Margo do whatever she wanted which was cry all the time and pray. Margo took no money from Jimmy, and he did have Kevin give it to her. Margo still had a third of the company which Tim still had shared through Linda and their daughter after Larry. But Jimmy had the most shares now because Jimmy had bought out the bank's shares.

Sue, Margo's mom, died in her sleep just before Christmas, which had Jimmy and Tim all upset. They were very close to Sue, and the funeral was quick and she was buried by her son, Jr. Joey, his wife, Jenny. Jimmy and Tim prayed a lot at the church with Margo crying uncontrollably. Mark was just too sad with Merit too.

Then after Christmas, Jimmy and Margo were seen talking together. Tim looked at Kevin but said nothing. Kevin didn't want to ask Jimmy about it. None of the guys would either. Then to all their surprise, Jimmy took Sarah, Michael, Margo, and Tim on vacation to Mexico. Kevin got a call from Tim saying get down to Mexico; Jimmy wants to adopt a little girl, make it happen and get the paperwork done, then come to Mexico and do it here. Kevin did as he was told. Jimmy and his family came home with a homeless girl about Tammy's age named Marie. This homeless child taught the family how to heal from the death of Tammy and about Halloween where you go to the grave site and have a party with the dead one. Jimmy loved this, and so did the kids. Marie also taught them about hot cocoa with cinnamon. Jimmy loved the taste of it. Marie, a child who had nothing, helped a family who had everything money could buy. What a beautiful thing to watch as the family with everything money could buy heal with Marie's help.

Margo moved back into the home and Jimmy remarried Margo one night alone. No one said a word about it and prayed the mess was over; they would never forget Tammy.

Aaron had some information about this Billy Joe person, and he was sure that Billy Joe had killed Marci and his brother, Daron had somehow found out, so Billy Joe had to kill him too. But how did Billy Joe kill Marci and Daron? Maybe Marci knew Billy Joe, and he was at that place, so she let him into the office, and he shot her, then ran away to hide. Daron was driving to Aaron's place, and somehow Billy Joe got into the car and drove it off the road then got out, not being seen. Kevin was not sure, no proof. But Kevin took it to Jimmy and to Jimmy it did make sense.

What all Jimmy said was that "Billy Joe just suddenly appeared in Marci's office and then disappeared again or we would have found him. Billy Joe just appeared in Daron's car and drove it off the road then poofed out of the driver's seat to safety." Kevin was not sure what Jimmy was talking about, but he had heard from others Jimmy was hard to understand so that must be it. They continue to work to find this Billy Joe, and then Tim called for Kevin again.

"Get over here. Margo is gone, kidnapped. They want one billion dollars for her, or they will kill her. Jimmy is very upset, and Sam will be staying here with the kids," Tim said. Kevin went over right away and left Aaron to find this Billy Joe, himself. Kevin looked at the note, something was just not right about it, but he couldn't put his figure on it. How did they get her? Nothing made sense to Kevin. The security system was working, and Sam was a mess over it. Jimmy agreed to pay the money, but they continued to look for Margo day and night until he paid the money. No police were called, just them, Jimmy, Tim, and Kevin were on it. T-Jay and Mickey with Merit and Mark ran the company as Aaron was still working on this Billy Joe.

Aaron came running to Kevin saying, "I have Billy Joe's home address." Jimmy just walked over and took it from Aaron's hands and was gone.

Tim said, "Can you take me to Jimmy, Kevin? I know he is at that address." Kevin looked confused, how in hell would he be able to do that? Then Tim said, "We can take the car."

Aaron went with and showed them the way and waited in the car as Tim and Kevin went inside to find Jimmy. As they walked in, Jimmy had his hands on some guy's neck, and the guy fell to the floor. Tim said, "We didn't see that. Nothing happened here." Tim then went to check if the guy had died. Margo came running out of the bedroom crying to Jimmy. They took Margo to the hospital and then Jimmy took the guy's body away but where? Jimmy was gone so fast.

Kevin and Aaron just sat there until Tim said, "Go back to the house and get the evidence. Billy Joe is who kidnapped Margo, killed Marci, and maybe Daron." Kevin and Aaron did just that, and Tim was right with all he had just said. There was no proof of how Billy Joe died. Tim said "He killed himself when they caught him. He hung himself in the house with no police there." But then there was no body. Jimmy took him to that place where Marci had lived. Maybe for her family to know he was dead and paid the price for killing Marci, but why? Jimmy checked it.

Jimmy said, "Margo had an abortion with Billy Joe's baby. Billy Joe killed Marci because Margo thought she knew about my other daughter and wouldn't tell her. Marci was going to tell me they were looking for the child. I have a daughter older than Sarah by Sylvia. I need to find my daughter, Teresa. Kevin, you are the only one to know. Tell no one. Daron died because he found out all of this and was going to tell you and Aaron about it. Daron was to find my kid." Kevin heard Jimmy but Aaron didn't, and he was standing right there. Kevin heard Jimmy in his head but didn't see Jimmy's mouth moving or heard words. What was going on, was he crazy?

Kevin told no one this. Tim appeared to know, and so did Jimmy. Aaron was pleased they got his brother's killer, and he died. Aaron didn't care how he died just that they killed him. An eye for an eye, Aaron told Kevin. Kevin was still a bit out of it. Then Jimmy told Kevin to get him a divorce from Margo again. So Kevin did, and Margo made no fuss about it. Margo told Tim that Billy Joe had raped her and that he wanted her to have the abortion because he was afraid Jimmy wouldn't pay the money if he knew Margo was pregnant with his child. Jimmy didn't believe any of this. So Margo moved back with Merit and Mark to live again. No one said a word about it, not even the gossipy employees. Then weeks later, Mark got sick and died in the hospital of cancer. No one said anything about it, and the funeral was small. Just Margo, Merit, Tim, and Jimmy. Kevin went too because he was security so Sam could have a day off. Sam took Margo's kidnapping very hard and blamed himself for not having the best security.

Tim said, "That Billy Joe got into Margo's car as he did Daron's" and Jimmy believed Tim. He didn't go through with the divorce this time. Margo came home, but things were not okay.

Kevin came into Jimmy's office one day, and Jimmy sang a song to himself, "I wish I didn't know now what I didn't know then. I wish I could start this all over again. You still have my heart in the palm of your hand." Then Jimmy stopped and looked at Kevin, saying, "What?"

Kevin said, "I think I am having a nervous breakdown. I saw gold things in my head or coming out of it. What is wrong with me? Help me." Kevin walked to the mirror and saw them again.

Tim came in and said, "Oh, Kevin, by the way, you are an alien from another planet and have gold antennas in your head. That is why you can hear Jimmy without talking to him. Jimmy is the leader of this planet. You know where we always went to see Marci? You can disappear and reappear at will, and you can read people's minds. Cool right? Sorry I am not an alien too."

Jimmy said to Tim, "Just stop it." Kevin had to lay down on the chair, and he felt sick. Now Kevin was sure he was losing his mind. Jimmy continued, "Kevin, go home and get some rest." Then Jimmy just walked out the door, and Kevin closed his eyes, to sleep. This had to be a bad dream. When Kevin opened his eyes, Tim was sitting there waiting for Kevin to be okay.

Tim said, "I think you could use a drink. Let us get drunk. Jimmy will not like it but what else is there to do about all this?" Kevin agreed, and they went to a bar and just drank all night.

In the morning Jimmy was mad, but he got a call and had to leave right away. Tim and Kevin's heads hurt, so they just drank coffee, very quietly. Kevin's wife was very mad at him, so he stayed with Tim and went home after she cooled down. Then Kevin went right to bed at home.

Jimmy called Tim and told him he would need a week off. Some of the children Jimmy and Marci had sponsored were killed in a gas leak on a ship home from George's place to where Marci and Jimmy had a home. Jimmy was very upset that Tim told the guys.

Kevin asked, "How many children does Jimmy sponsor this way? And is Jimmy ever going to replace Marci at the work, wherever that place is?" All the guys waited for Tim's answer.

Tim said, "Oh, I think a few thousand, maybe ten thousand by now. I don't know if Jimmy will ever replace Marci. I think Jimmy's kids help him with it all. They are little geniuses."

Jimmy was gone a few weeks, and Sam with Aaron watched Margo and the kids. But the kids didn't miss Jimmy, it was like he came back at night to put them to bed, but how? When Jimmy got back, he was different. He went places without anyone with him. Margo came crying in the office to Tim. Margo said, "Jimmy is having an affair with another woman, I know."

Tim said, "Okay, I don't believe it, but I will ask Kevin and Aaron to follow Jimmy and see." Margo agreed with that. So Kevin and Aaron stayed to follow Jimmy right to Aaron's house. In the window, they saw Jimmy having sex with Aaron's wife. Aaron was very upset about it. They told Margo, and she was getting a different lawyer than Kevin to divorce Jimmy over this. Tim still didn't believe and said, "I need to talk with Jimmy on this. You didn't see it, correct?"

In the morning, Aaron walked right up to Jimmy at work in front of all the employees and asked, "Are you sleeping with my wife, Jimmy?" No one said a word; you could have heard a pin drop.

Jimmy replied, "Yes, I am." Then Jimmy just walked away from Aaron. Aaron's wife,

April, filed for divorce from Aaron so she could marry Jimmy. Tim was speechless for the first time in his life. Aaron asked Margo to marry him, and they would show those two. Margo wanted to marry before Jimmy and April did. The divorce went well; Jimmy gave Margo whatever she wanted. Jimmy just said to Kevin, "Get me my freedom with shared control of my kids and Tim." So Kevin did what Jimmy told him to. The guys said nothing, but had a bet on how long Jimmy would stay married to April. Kevin bet six months it would last. Jimmy didn't appear to care what anyone thought or said. Tim cried.

At Margo and Aaron's wedding, Jimmy came alone without April, and he made a toast. Jimmy said, "Here is to the bride, my ex-wife and Aaron. Aaron, you took her away from me, and if you ever bring her back to me, I will kill you. She is yours forever. Good luck." Then Jimmy walked out the door and Margo with Aaron was less upset over Jimmy being there. Tim cried more. Merit did nothing; he was still too upset over Mark's death to even know what was happening. All the guys left with Jimmy. Jimmy's wedding to April was very small, not even his kids were there, just a Judge and not a pastor. Kevin and Tim were there, but Jimmy got drunk, but why?

Jimmy and April fought all the time, and in six months, April filed for divorce from Jimmy, but April wanted a lot of money. She had forgotten the pre-nuptial she sign that if the marriage didn't last a year, she got nothing. So April tried to make the divorce last over another six months.

Jimmy and Margo were fighting about the kids or Tim again, which one's turn it was to have them live in their homes. Jimmy lived at the house that Marci had with him. Jimmy's mother was there too, and Margo did like her, and she loved Margo. What a mess. Then things got worse as they always do. Jimmy and Margo had been fighting as Jimmy went to see her. Tim called Kevin into Jimmy's office, and Tim said, "Jimmy, tell Kevin what he needs to do for you today." Tim was laughing so hard he was laying on the floor laughing until he cried.

Jimmy said, "Kevin, I need you to go and tell this guy that I got his wife pregnant. I will give him one billion dollars if he doesn't have sex with her until my baby is born."

Kevin said, "You what? How will I know the guy? How will we enforce this? I won the bet on your last marriage." Tim was still laughing so hard that he couldn't add his two cents.

Then Tim said, "It is not how you will know the guy. It is who the guy is? Jimmy, is there something Margo has that you can't live without?"

Jimmy replied, "It is Aaron. Margo and I are going to have a baby. Aaron is an honorable guy, if he gives his word, I will trust him. Now please go and do it. No more talk about it."

Kevin wanted to say are you sure it is yours but he did as Jimmy told him to and to

Kevin's surprise Aaron had already known. He was not happy about it, but Margo was, and Aaron did need the money to complete the house Margo had to build for them.

Tim told everyone at work; the guys didn't know what to say so they said nothing and gave Kevin the money he won from the bet on how long Jimmy would stay married to April. Kevin was going to tell Jimmy that if the divorce takes longer than the marriage lasted that was very bad, but April killed herself over Margo having Jimmy's baby. Aaron was upset but what could he have done? Jimmy was sad too and said, "I never wanted that to happen to her, I just wanted my freedom from her. I would have given her money but nothing unreasonable."

Jimmy was very nice to Margo as she carried his baby and was at Jimmy's home all the time. Aaron was like the third wheel. Jimmy was very nice to Aaron, but Tim slept in the middle of Margo and Aaron when she even slept at home. Most of the time she was staying at Jimmy's.

Work continued at the business and Jimmy just acted like nothing was different. Jimmy did still go places without anyone. Was he seeing another woman or was Margo and Jimmy meeting for something else? No one said a word and Aaron knew they were all laughing at him, but he loved Margo so much now, what could he do? Aaron was sure after the baby was born and he got all that money, Margo would be pleased with the house he had to build for her, and they would start a family too. Aaron's dreams came true, and Margo gave birth to a baby girl for Jimmy. Tim delivered the baby, and all was good. Jimmy named the baby girl, Cindy Sue Elgin.

Jimmy was going to leave the company and start a new business. Jimmy would take only Kevin with and not any of the other guys for six months, then Margo and Aaron should be on their feet to run the company themselves with Merit. The guys were not pleased, but they agreed. Tim could go back and forth, for he never worked anymore anyway. Linda was lost but stayed with Margo. Jimmy took his baby girl to live with him and his mother in that place where Marci had once lived. Margo moved into her new home and Sarah, Michael with Marie lived in the house Jimmy had built so long ago for them. Jimmy thought it was best for the kids to stay in their home with the white-haired people to care for them. Margo was okay with this, and still was with Jimmy most of the time.

Tim said, "I am sure Jimmy and Margo will be back together again soon. We want Jimmy to have more children so let us put pin holes in his protection. I will take his billfold tonight and let's go to the bar and do it. Don't tell anyone. Genius should have more children, only dumb people are having all the kids. What is the world coming to?" Kevin agreed but his wife, Alice, told Kevin if he went out drinking she would burn all his things in the front yard. Now that was like a challenge to Kevin, so you know, if he just had to go drinking with Tim. And the more they drank, the more they thought this was a good idea. Then Tim said, "I got to get Jimmy's billfold back before he wakes up and finds out. Can you get home by yourself?"

Kevin said, "Yes, I will call a cab." And he did.

The cab driver asked, "Which one of the mansions is yours?"

Kevin said, "The one with the stuff burning in the front yard. I think you should take me to my workplace. Maybe this is not a good time to come home to the wife after having a few drinks."

The cab driver laughed and took Kevin to work. Kevin went to sleep in his chair, but before he knew it, Jimmy was there waking him up. Jimmy said, "Kevin I need your help."

Kevin replied, "More lawyer work?"

Jimmy answered, "No, get in your plane. I have to bomb the hell out of a country today. So you fly them away from me so I can do that, okay?"

Kevin asked, "Wouldn't that make them mad and want to kill me?"

Jimmy answered, "Yes, but you can poof out of your plane to be safe. We have to go now."

Kevin was not sure of this, but he did as Jimmy told him to. As Kevin flew his plane away from Jimmy, the other planes followed him as Jimmy said they would, and started shooting at Kevin. But Kevin had no idea how to poof out, and no one had told him that you could not pilot drunk. Kevin's plane got hit, and he was going down fast. At the last minute, a pretty strawberry blonde poofed Kevin out of there to safety where they hid together until Jimmy came for Kevin.

Jimmy came for Kevin and said, "Kevin, be sure to thank the girl for saving your life. Ask if there is anything you could do for her. Now go talk with her, hurry back, we have to get out of here."

Kevin went to the girl and said "Thank you so much for saving my life. Is there anything at all I could do for you?"

The girl giggled and answered, "I could use some sex from you." Now, to Kevin that sounded fair. Kevin was sure from the burning of his things in the front yard, his wife was there.

Kevin replied, "Okay, I am always up for sex. Jimmy, can I have some of your protection? I didn't stop at the drug store this morning before we left. I will need a few hours to do my best."

Jimmy answered, "What the hell? Okay, Kevin, do what you need to do, and here is some protection from my billfold. But you got thirty minutes and no more so get to it." Kevin started thinking billfold, but then he remembered he only had thirty minutes to please the lady, so he did.

After thirty minutes, Kevin got into Jimmy's plane to go home, and not a word. Kevin did sleep most of the way but when he got home Kevin's wife threw her arms around

Kevin and wanted to make love to him. So Kevin turned to Jimmy and Jimmy took his money out and threw his billfold at Kevin. No words were said. Tim came later but all was good, and Kevin was asleep. Tim said, "That must have been hard work for Kevin. The boy is fast asleep."

Jimmy replied, "You don't know the half of it." Jimmy was not happy, but Kevin was until later.

Kevin wife, Alice, wanted to go out to eat at a romantic place for Valentine's day. Before they got their food, Alice said, "Kevin, we are going to have a baby." Kevin wanted to ask is it mine? But he was just too upset that she had the nerve to tell him before he got to eat and he was not hungry now. Kevin thought for a minute, what was the right answer to this statement?

Then Kevin said, "My love. This child is a gift from God because I used protection and you got pregnant anyway. Please take care of yourself and see Tim right away for good health." Kevin knew that he was so full of it, but he didn't think God would get him for this, but who knows. Alice was happy, calling her parents and Kevin's with the good news.

The next day, it was even worse for Kevin, as he walked in Jimmy called to Kevin, "Come in here now." So Kevin did and sat down. Jimmy replied, "Remember your plane issue and the strawberry blonde? Well, she is pregnant, and I am sure it is yours. You better take care of her or I will have to kill you. Now here is her address and her name is Grace. Go and don't fail."

Kevin got up to go, but he said, "Good one, God, you got me good. Two women are pregnant on the same day. Oh shit, I remember now, pin hole in Jimmy's protection, and then I used them."

Tim replied, "Praying out loud, Kevin, not a good plan." T-Jay, Sam, and Mickey were laughing. Tim turned to Mickey and said, "Stop laughing, your wife is pregnant too."

Mickey replied, "Not possible, she is on the pill."

Tim said, "Funny thing about that pill, the woman has to take it, or it doesn't work. You can't trust a woman to do that. You're going to be a father, Mickey." Mickey just cried.

T-Jay said, "That is why I got myself fixed. What about you, Sam?"

Sam replied, "I never want to talk about my kids ever. When they are twenty-one, I will be okay."

Kevin left for Grace's place. It looked like he was not the only unhappy married guy. At Grace's, Kevin just told her the truth that Jimmy would kill him unless she let him pay for everything and helps care for their child. Kevin promised to be there always but told her he is married with a child. Grace was very nice, and they wrote up an agreement. Grace would tell the child Kevin was the father. They would be truthful to the child and each other. It didn't go as good as it sounded. The women were hard to get along with, and they wanted sex 24/7. Tim gave Kevin vitamins as he did the women. None of the guys felt sorry for Kevin, even when he told them how hard this was for him. He wasn't getting any sleep and the food he had to get those women was unbelievable. Kevin went out day and night, he couldn't even work, but Jimmy was okay with that. Where was Jimmy going alone all the time?

Tim said, "Kevin, as soon as your women have your babies, you need to follow Jimmy again."

Kevin replied, "Can't the other guys follow Jimmy this time?" The guys shook their heads, no.

Kevin was sure he needed mental therapy from the last time he saw Jimmy having sex with April. How could he do this again? And who would help him? Surely not Aaron. Then things got worse as they always do. The two women were ready to have the babies. Grace went in first, and Kevin drove her to the hospital for Tim to deliver the baby with Jimmy's help. Kevin decided to have both women at the same hospital because he was sure they would both have the babies on the same day. Tim laughed and said, "Kevin, my boy that just will not happen." But Tim, their doctor was wrong. The minute Kevin got Grace to the hospital, Alice called him to take her to the hospital. Kevin was so tired of all the driving, and he told the guys who didn't feel sorry in the least for him. Then Kevin had to walk back and forth between the rooms. Kevin's back was killing him, and he told Jimmy who was not feeling sorry for him.

Jimmy said, "Kevin, think about what those women have to do. How much this hurts." Kevin was sure he had the worst of it, he thought, but the women were screaming and calling him bad names.

Then Grace gave birth to a baby girl. Kevin named her, Betsy Grace Carlson. Then Grace died. In the agreement they wrote up, dying was not in the plan. Grace looked up at Kevin holding his baby girl and closed her eyes. Kevin was too upset to think. He knew nothing about kids. Tim had to go to Alice who gave Kevin a baby boy. Kevin named him Calvin Kevin Carlson. But Alice didn't die. Kevin said to Tim, "Let Alice died, and I'll keep Grace."

Tim sat Kevin down and said, "I am sorry, it just doesn't work that way."

Jimmy, Kevin, and little Betsy took Grace to bury her where Jimmy had a place by Marci's grave. Kevin cried and said, "What am I going to do?"

Jimmy replied, "Tell Alice the truth." Kevin was sure that would never work on Alice.

Kevin went to Tim, and Tim said, "Tell Alice she had twins. I gave her a lot of drugs for the pain. I can write it out on the birth papers, but if anyone looks close, they will see the truth." Then Tim had to go because Mickey's wife was having her baby. What a day or two. Mickey's wife had a baby boy; she named Micky Mickey Johnson. Mickey just cried.

Kevin got a nurse to watch the babies and Alice wanted nothing to do with these babies or Kevin. So Kevin slept in the babies' room with the nurse. Kevin had the nurse wear little tiny swimsuits. It was just a hop or skip away, and Kevin was sleeping with the nurse. One morning Alice found Kevin in bed with the nurse, and she threw Kevin with the nurse out. Alice had to take the babies to the doctor for their exams and found that the girl was not hers. Then Alice filed for divorce from Kevin because Kevin cheated on her with Betsy's mom and the nurse.

Kevin was a good divorce lawyer, but there was no way he could come out ahead on this one. Kevin even tried to sleep with the divorce Judge but Alice must have gotten to her first, Kevin told everyone. Jimmy, Tim, and the guys did feel sorry for Kevin as he sat in his office waiting for Alice to come to take Calvin away from him. Kevin sat there with little Betsy and Calvin crying and praying for God's help. Kevin even got confession with God about his sins, promising to stop.

Alice, now Kevin's ex-wife just had to have these thousand dollar shoes to wear. Kevin didn't want his ex-wife to go without shoes, but two thousand dollars for a pair of shoes was to Kevin, a little over the top. But he lost big in the divorce court. What could Kevin say about his cheating, that he and his wife were apart with Betsy's mom and his lying about Alice having twins or the sleeping with the babies' nurse? All was not good for Kevin, as Alice came with the divorce papers for Kevin to sign and then everything he had ever had was now hers. Even all his cars he loved so much, the house, and most of all his son, Calvin. Jimmy had told Kevin that he and Betsy could live with him and Cindy. Jimmy had built a new house with a place for Tim with Linda. Linda was not happy with Margo. Margo was mean to everyone even Aaron. Linda would help Kevin with his daughter, Besty. Kevin was thinking this all over as Alice came.

Alice said, "Give my son to me, Calvin. You can have visiting times as I see fit. And I better get your paycheck in time. Sign the divorce papers and send them in as soon as possible." Alice took Calvin from Kevin's arms and Betsy was with Kevin, crying. Alice left the room with Calvin. Kevin heard a loud sound and Calvin was crying. Kevin, with Betsy in his arms, ran to see what was wrong. There laid Alice on the stairs. Her eyes were open wide, but she was not talking. That was a first, Alice not talking, she must be dead, Kevin thought. Tim and Jimmy came running to see what happened. Tim checked Alice and Jimmy called for an ambulance. But Alice died. She got her high heel of those two thousand dollar shoes caught on the rug from the stairs and hit her head when she fell backward. Calvin was not hurt at all but crying. As they took Alice away, Kevin thanked God and got on his knees to pray for Kevin knew he didn't have to sign the divorce papers. Kevin could keep everything of his, and that were Calvin too. At the time of death, Alice and Kevin were legally married.

Kevin was more than happy to pay for Alice's funeral and even sold their house giving that money to her parents. Kevin had Alice's parent decide where to have Alice buried. All Kevin wanted was for them to treat Betsy as they did Calvin, like a grandchild. Kevin had paperwork on it, and he would take the kids to see their grandparents as often as they wanted, both Alice's and his parents. But both parents did believe Kevin or Jimmy or one of the guys had killed Alice.

Kevin asked the guys but not Jimmy, "Did any of you kill my soon to be ex-wife? I would not be mad if you did, tell me." But they all said that they had nothing to do with it and were still working at Margo's company. But their six months were up, and they were all back with Jimmy at his new business. With all that money, Aaron should be able to get the company going good, and Margo was pregnant with twin boys from Aaron or was it Jimmy's again? Tim did check it out, the baby boys were Aaron's and when they were born, Margo named them Merit Tim Elgin Erup and Mark Joey Elgin Erup.

Kevin moved in with Jimmy with his kids. Linda took care of Kevin's children, and Kevin was just Kevin, doing as little as possible with Tim. Jimmy had his new business up and going good, enough work for the guys. T-Jay, Sam, and Mickey were glad to be back with Jimmy.

CHAPTER SEVEN

CINDY ELGIN PETERSON, THE SILVER ONE

One day, Tim asked Jimmy, "Why did you marry April? The two of you never even knew each other. Did someone kill April for you, so you didn't have to go through a divorce?" Jimmy was playing with his children, and Cindy was enjoying being with her dad as she always did. Cindy followed Jimmy everywhere. Michael was with Marie all the time, and Sarah had many boyfriends which worried Jimmy.

Jimmy replied, "Because I thought Margo wanted Aaron when I came back from that trip with the kids I sponsored. I was sure Margo was in love with Aaron, and I knew Aaron would never be untrue to anyone. I also knew April loved money and I could charm her into marrying me. Then she would divorce me. A guy can't walk away from a woman safely. She will come after him until his dying day, but if the woman left the man? That was the only thing guys can do." Tim thought that Jimmy gave Margo everything, even Aaron, if Jimmy believed Margo wanted him. Tim was sure Margo made a big mistake and was being unreasonable. So Tim just drank more and so did Margo. Even when Margo had the twins she never stopped drinking.

Jimmy started coming over to T-Jay's home when T-Jay was at work with Cindy. Was Sally babysitting for Jimmy while he worked or what was going on? Kevin followed him. T-Jay didn't know what to think, but Jimmy was very happy, and they all just thought the worst. Sally said nothing to T-Jay about it, and he was afraid to ask. The question was, who was going to ask Jimmy if he was sleeping with T-Jay's wife, Sally? Then out of nowhere, Jimmy called T-Jay into his office with Sally there. They all were sure they knew what was happening. But they were all wrong. T-Jay later wished it had been Jimmy sleeping with Sally, but it was not. Sally had cancer and Jimmy was her doctor. Jimmy had her cancer under control, but now Sally was dying from it, and they had to tell T-Jay. Jimmy was a mess that he had failed to help someone as nice as Sally. If Jimmy was so smart and a genius then why could he not save Sally's life?

It was a big funeral, but then he had a lot of practice with funerals. T-Jay was a mess, and so was Jimmy. Sam and Mickey were there for T-Jay, but Jimmy wanted to be alone, so after the funeral Kevin and Tim just got drunk. Margo and Aaron didn't even come to

Sally's funeral. Jimmy started dating a model. He liked having sex with her in the limo. The model loved Jimmy, but as fast as it started, Jimmy ended it with this model. Kevin and Tim never got the name of the woman, it didn't last that long. What was up with Jimmy? Tim found out the model Jimmy was dating wanted to marry Jimmy and have children. Jimmy didn't want any more children, and that was that so he got her mad so she would break it off with him.

Jimmy and Margo were always fighting again over the money, Margo always wanted money from Jimmy, and she made it hard for Jimmy with the kids or having Tim live with him.

Jimmy made out a Will and left everything to Cindy. Kevin asked, "What about the other kids?"

Jimmy replied, "Michael will get this house for him and Marie that I had built for Margo. Sarah will get this building for her work on oceans which Sarah loves to do. But Cindy is so little, and I am getting older, what if I am not here for her growing up? She will need money and other things to complete her education. Michael is well on his way to being a doctor and Marie, his nurse, is always at Michael's side. Sarah's training in oceans. I have paid for that education."

Kevin did the Will for Jimmy, and Margo found out about it and wanted money, or she would take Jimmy to court for control of Cindy. Margo said, "Any Judge would understand a little girl needs her mommy." Margo would also be asking for child support for Cindy. The other kids the Judge would let give their input on who they wanted to live with and it was Jimmy. Had Margo and Aaron spent all the billions of dollars Jimmy had given them and then what about the divorce money Margo got from Jimmy, as he gave her whatever money she wanted?

Kevin was also being sued by that nurse for emotional harm. She said Kevin hurt her by not loving her in the papers for the court. Kevin replied in writing that he just had sex with her and there was no love involved. Kevin didn't even know the woman's name. Kevin asked for a trial by jury and not in this area which the Judge did agree to.

Jimmy had Kevin as his lawyer in Margo's custody lawsuit for Cindy. Kevin whispered to Jimmy, "Let Margo's lawyers go first. Let's see what they do." Margo's lawyer's input was very basic that a little girl should be with her mother. Margo was now a stay home mother with her twin boys and could care better for Cindy than Jimmy, a working father. Then Margo's lawyer added Jimmy's sex life with the model in his limo and the death of Jimmy's second wife, April.

Kevin's defense that Jimmy had Cindy from birth and that there were legal papers on the fact for Jimmy to have Cindy in his sole care. Jimmy had paid Margo and Aaron one billion dollars for Margo to have his child. Then Jimmy handed Kevin a DNA report showing Margo just carried the baby and gave birth to Cindy but was not the biological mother.

Margo's lawyer reviewed it all, but it was all there. Billion dollars was a lot of money to pay for this, but this kind of arrangement was not unheard of by the rich and famous. The Judge reviewed Jimmy's Will and papers on this arrangement then ruled in favor of Jimmy.

Margo screamed at the Judge, "Jimmy was an alien from another planet." The judge ruled Margo would never get any of Jimmy's or their children. Margo needed mental health care. Aaron took Margo home before the Judge would take their twins away from Margo. Jimmy said nothing to anyone.

Kevin's, lawsuit with this nurse, who had watched his kids, came to an end when her plane and all her money sucking lawyers went down and burned to the ground before their case went to court. Kevin just got down on his knee and prayed. Had someone done something to that plane?

Margo started drinking more, and she left Tim to do whatever he wanted to do, which was also to drink. Aaron had no control, but to raise his sons; he tried to run the company, which was losing more money every day. So, Jimmy agreed to give Margo and Aaron another billion dollars if Margo and Tim went into rehab to do the treatment program to stop drinking. Margo agreed and had Tim go with her into rehab. Kevin missed Tim, but he did what Jimmy told him to. Tim would be out in about six weeks, it was not that long, and would be home for Thanksgiving. Jimmy paid the money and on Thanksgiving, Margo and Tim had completed the program. Now it was up to them to go to the AA meetings and not drink at all. Tim stayed his first night home at Jimmy's place as in the contract written by Kevin and signed by Margo. Jimmy would now have control of Tim and his kids forever. Margo and Aaron had the money. All was good.

But that morning of Thanksgiving, Linda left early to help Margo cook, and Tim was still in bed. Jimmy just let Tim sleep until it was time to go to Margo and Aaron's. Jimmy said to Kevin, "Go in and wake Tim and make sure he's dressed so we can go. I'll get the kids." Kevin went into Tim's room, but Tim was laying there with a bottle of wine almost all gone. Tim didn't move at all.

Kevin cried, "Jimmy come here. Something is wrong with Tim. He is not moving and is cold." Jimmy ran into Tim's room and tried everything, but Tim had died. Jimmy poofed Tim away with him to someplace, but there was nothing Jimmy could do. Tim had died that Thanksgiving. Margo blamed Jimmy for Tim's death. Mickey, Kevin, and Jimmy took it very hard with Linda. But T-Jay and Sam didn't care. When Merit heard of his dad, Tim's death, he drove his car into a tree and died right away with no pain. Merit loved his dad so much and couldn't go on.

Now the funeral was sad, and they had seen some sad funerals but Tim with Merit buried at the same time was not good. Margo screamed at Jimmy the whole time. Kevin and Mickey couldn't even talk. Aaron had his hands full with Margo. Jimmy didn't have the kids come and paid for everything. Tim and Merit buried by Tammy, Travis, and James, Jimmy's kids. Jimmy cried just as hard as Kevin and Mickey. Kevin took care of Linda, Tim's wife after that.

Jimmy had Mickey, Kevin, and the guys read letters Tim wrote to them while in rehab. Jimmy had read his letter alone by Tim's grave. Then Jimmy said to Kevin and Mickey, "We have to go on. We have our children to raise. Tim was my best friend and will always be that to me." Jimmy took Mickey and Kevin to Tim's old house where he grew up. They had once lived there with many happy times. Jimmy wanted to restore the house to what it looked like when Tim was growing up in it with his mom and dad. They would do the work themselves and hire guys to show them how to do it. The work would help them heal from Tim's death. Jimmy was sure all the townspeople would want to remember Tim. Tim had helped them all so much. Tim's house would be a place to visit to remember Tim always. So they worked as T-Jay and Sam ran the new business for Jimmy. They took their time on the work and found many things of Tim's in the house to laugh about remembering Tim. It did help with the healing of Tim's death.

They found something on the floor about Sylvia and a daughter which Jimmy had left in his old bedroom. Jimmy said, "Kevin, I need you to help me find my older daughter, Teresa." Then Jimmy made a few new rules if you are going to work for him you couldn't drink any liquor even off the job, no smoking or drug use unless by a doctor for medication. The guys agreed and signed the paper Kevin wrote up for the new business. No one would drink after Tim's death.

In a small container, Tim had left Kevin DNA of Sylvia and wrote that Jimmy might think a woman is her but test her first because they never are Sylvia. Jimmy had a problem with this. Tim also requested that Kevin take care of Jimmy as long as Jimmy would live. Kevin would.

Margo and Aaron had lost the company over too many unpaid bills. I guess a billion dollars doesn't go as far as it once did or was Margo on drugs? On drugs, anyone can go through money so fast that it feels like nothing at all. Even a billion dollars is just up in the air and gone. Margo wanted more money from Jimmy, but he just said, "No. I am pleased Tim is not here to see the company he worked so hard go under because of Margo's drug use. Margo is a woman I gave everything to, and she throws it all away for what? Drugs and more drugs."

It was true, Margo had been a beautiful woman with diamonds and everything, who now had nothing. Margo's face was inward and her clothes never good, it's so sad to see this happen.

It was the Christmas after Tim had died and somehow Margo got into the house. Jimmy was in the shower. Margo took her gun and shot him in the chest. Margo was trying for a shot to Jimmy's heart. He fell, but Kevin was in there in a flash with a blanket over Jimmy and to Michael, he poofed Jimmy. Michael did get the bullet out right away, and there was little bleeding. Jimmy would be okay. Sam had Margo and was going to call the police, but Jimmy said, "Don't do that Sam, just call Aaron to come and go." Sam did what Jimmy wanted and called Aaron. Did Jimmy still love Margo or was it because she was the mother of his kids? Jimmy would not press charges against Margo, but he did ask for security and that Margo was never to come to his home again. Kevin would stay with Jimmy 24/7 or Sam would take over. Kevin would even sleep in the same room with Jimmy but not the same bed. And the bathroom, Jimmy said was off limits to everyone, if he was in there. All agreed, but they watched Jimmy closely. No one was going to kill their boss. Not now or ever. The guys were on it with Kevin.

Cindy started asking questions about who her parents were. Jimmy was having the guys watch this movie called the Da Vinci code about Jesus being married to Mary and having a daughter named Sarah. Did Jesus have a bloodline and why were they watching it? Kevin was sure Jimmy would explain, but he never did. Cindy with her friends, Betsy, Calvin, and Micky hid upstairs and watched the movie too. Cindy was sure Jimmy was the grand master and knew the secret. Was Jimmy even her father? So as in the movie, Cindy went through Jimmy's desk. Jimmy walked and said, "Cindy what are you doing on my desk? Need something, money?"

Cindy replied, "Are you mad at me? Are you going to send me away? Are you the grandmaster?"

Jimmy answered. "I am not mad at you. I am not going to send you away. And who's grandmaster is this?"

Cindy said, "In the movie you had the guys watch. Are you my real father?"

Jimmy started to laugh but tried not to and said, "That is just a movie about a book, nothing more. I am your real father. Come, let's have Michael do a DNA test right now." So they went to Michael, and he did the test with Cindy being Jimmy's biological daughter without any question.

Cindy was happy for a short time, but then she got the papers from the court with Margo being only her birth mother and not her biological mother. Was Cindy from a test tube or what? Was this Marci her mother? Or did her mother try to have an abortion with her and Jimmy found out then saved her? Cindy's mind was working overtime on this. Cindy went to Jimmy and asked, "Who is my real mother? Did I come from a test tube? Or was she going to have an abortion with me? What happened? Why was I put in Margo? Who did that to me?"

Jimmy sat back, his face was all red, he answered, "Can I have some time to answer all your question. You are not a test tube baby. You're like most babies are made. Your mother didn't have, or try to have, an abortion with you. I put you in Margo because I ran out of time. Can we talk about this when you are a little older? I love your mother very much, and she loves you. I am looking for your mother, and I will bring her to you as soon as I find her. I need her too." Kevin walked in to help Jimmy and see if Cindy would stop questioning her dad about her mom. Kevin motioned for Cindy to leave because they both knew Jimmy would tell Cindy no more, but maybe he would tell Kevin, so Cindy went out but listened at the door. Calvin, Betsy, and Micky came to be with Cindy and to help find out who her biological mother was.

Kevin said, "Don't you remember Cindy's mom's name? Well, who were you having sex with at the time? Why did you use Margo of all people to carry Cindy and give birth to her?"

Jimmy replied, "Yes, I do remember who Cindy's mom is and her name. I have only had sex with seven women in my life. Margo had called to tell me about the kids, Sarah, Michael, and Marie. I was afraid if I didn't go to Margo that she might hurt one of them like what happened to Tammy. Sally, T-Jay's wife, was going to carry the baby for us, but Sally was sick and couldn't. That's how we found out Sally had cancer. Cindy's mom couldn't carry her after problems when our son died. I thought she had died, but you found out she was still alive with my daughter Teresa. We have to find my daughter and then I will find my true love, Cindy's mom. Cindy looks so much like her physical mom, and I miss her so much. I need her."

Kevin didn't know what to say, but at least Cindy knew her mother loved her and Jimmy was still in love with Cindy's mother. Now all they had to do was find her and bring her to Jimmy.

Kevin started looking for Jimmy's daughter, Teresa. She had been a waitress in a café, so Kevin went to eat at all the cafés looking for a waitresses named Teresa. Jimmy also wrote down Teresa had a daughter and was married, but he didn't know anymore. No one knows how long Kevin did this, but Kevin did love to eat out and date waitresses. Sometimes Kevin took his kids with, but Kevin never noticed there was one more kid, Mickey's son, Micky. How could Kevin not noticed three kids where there should have been only two, but Kevin missed that one.

One week did stand out for attention, the week Kevin took off with his kids to be with a waitress, but Jimmy thought nothing of it because Kevin said her name was not Teresa. She did have a daughter.

Kevin had a romantic week with this waitress and Calvin fell in love with the little daughter. Calvin couldn't see her again because Kevin forgot the waitress' name. He did give her his real name and phone number. To Kevin's surprise this waitress never called him, but why?

T-Jay was having a problem with Jimmy's daughter, Sarah. She was looking at him, and he was afraid of her. Sarah had grown up, and she had the biggest crush on T-Jay. She would even flirt with him. T-Jay didn't know what to do, and when Sarah came close to him, T-Jay would drop anything in his hands. Sam appeared to be a little jealous. Mickey laughed.

T-Jay knocked on Jimmy's bedroom door and asked, "Can I talk with you?" Kevin was up walking around. No one was going to hurt his boss. Jimmy was going to live forever.

Jimmy replied, "Can't it wait until morning?" T-Jay didn't answer so Jimmy said, "Come in if you must and tell me what you want at this hour. We can do Sally's home like we did Tim's if that is what you need to ask me. You and Sam can work on it, and we'll take over at the business."

T-Jay said, "Yes, I would like to do that, but I am not here to talk about that. My problem is, well, your kids are a great boss and growing up so fast. Sarah is very smart, but she touched my arm and my face with her hand. I don't think that is okay." Jimmy sat up in bed.

Jimmy asked, "Is my daughter, Sarah, coming on to you, T-Jay?" T-Jay got all red in his face. Sam looked at the door.

Mickey said, "Yes, boss, she is big time coming on to T-Jay." Jimmy's eyes opened wide and looked at Kevin who just shrugged.

Jimmy said, "Thank you for telling me this. I will take care of it in the morning. Don't worry."

T-Jay asked, "Am I fired?" Jimmy shook his head no. They all left, and Jimmy tried to sleep. In the morning Jimmy had breakfast with Sarah, and they talked. Sarah loved the color white and T-Jay, so Jimmy decided to send Sarah away to a college with boys her age. Sarah cried about it, but she went. Things were back to normal, and T-Jay wasn't dropping stuff. Sarah did come home on the weekend and then she was talking with T-Jay who didn't know what to do.

Jimmy had spoiled his children, and Kevin was no better. Kevin had no idea how to raise a kid. But Kevin prayed about it daily and so did Jimmy. They were guys trying to raise children and daughters too. Then things got worse on Thanksgiving. Linda didn't come out of her room, so Kevin went in and found Linda had died in her sleep. That Linda was dead was very hard for Kevin's kids for this was the only mother Calvin and Betsy had ever known. The funeral was small and Margo didn't go. Aaron called Jimmy to meet with him after the funeral. Jimmy questioned why, but thought maybe it was about Linda's funeral, so he agreed to meet Aaron at an out of the way apartment, where Aaron's dad lived. Jimmy had nothing against Aaron's dad.

Kevin said, "Boss, I am going with you. Don't disagree with me about it." Jimmy nodded in agreement, and they left. When they got there, Jimmy went to the door alone. Kevin watched carefully and saw Aaron had a gun at his side out of sight for Jimmy to see. Aaron raised the gun to shoot Jimmy. Kevin rushed there to push Aaron down. The gun went off and shot Jimmy in the foot. Kevin whisked Jimmy over to Michael for care. Michael was upset. But again Jimmy would not file a police report against Aaron. Jimmy did talk to the police about it and went to see someone, but he was sure that wouldn't help.

Jimmy said, "I made the mistake of trusting and going to see Aaron. I wanted this to stop, but now I know it never will. Margo will blame me for all kind of unreasonable things that I couldn't have done. Some fools may even believe her, but most will laugh behind her back. What we need is more security." Jimmy was sure Margo and Aaron just wanted him dead for the money, and that was all there was to it. Just greed and drug money with liquor also used, but Margo didn't see it.

Sam's son and daughter wanted to work security, so Jimmy hired them right away. Jimmy said, "I want to hire C-Jay to watch Cindy. She is the one Margo wants because of the money." Sam went to talk with C-Jay, and he was a little afraid to watch Cindy. All the guys could not say no to Jimmy, so he agreed. C-Jay was nervous around Cindy, and she noticed.

Cindy said to Jimmy, "Dad, I think C-Jay hates me. Please don't ask him to be my security. I can take care of myself. I hate Margo and Aaron for what they have done to you."

Jimmy smiled and said, "Hate is a big word. Let me talk with C-Jay and see what the issue is. Is C-Jay nice to you or not?"

Cindy replied, "C-Jay is very nice to me, a perfect gentleman at all times." Jimmy just smiled.

Jimmy called C-Jay into his office and said, "I bet the animals on the farm have all had their babies and winter is coming on. Could you and your grandparents use some help with making a warm place for all those babies? I know now that you are helping me with security it takes time away from helping on the farm. Why don't you take Cindy, Betsy, Calvin, and Micky with you this weekend to help on the farm? It would be good for the kids to get away from all issues."

C-Jay agreed with Jimmy as he always did, and that weekend took the kids with him to the farm. Jimmy told the kids, "Remember, you are guests at the farm and be respectful to C-Jay's grandparents at all times. The farm is not the city or the castle you live in, make do." The kids agreed and were so pleased to go to the farm. Calvin was not so upset about not seeing the little girl he loves, and Kevin didn't know her name or anything. Calvin had a lot of questions about how the farm worked. Betsy loved cooking with grandma. Micky liked helping grandma in the garden with the vegetables. Cindy just loved the animals on the farm.

From then on C-Jay talked more with Cindy and they became good friends. Weekends on the farm was a thing the kids did every weekend from then on. Calvin was still mad at Kevin. Jimmy and Kevin went looking for his oldest daughter, and they were driving in the capital of the new state they had moved to that month. As they were driving, Jimmy said, "Stop the car." And Jimmy jumped out of the car. Kevin parked the car and went after Jimmy. Jimmy had followed a blonde hair woman who bounced all over when she walked into this place and was dancing with her. Jimmy's foot had healed, and he danced all night with that woman. Kevin just sat there and ate food. Then the woman wanted to go home, so Jimmy walked her to her car. It was a black sports car but not the same one in the videos. She wouldn't give Jimmy her phone number, so he gave her his and told her to call him anytime. She drove away, and Jimmy just stood there like a fool. No one talked on the way home. Kevin was glad Jimmy had a good time dancing with the woman. Kevin had never seen Jimmy act that way around anyone else.

Jimmy waited by the phone day and night, but she never called him. Then they went looking for her. Kevin asked as they were looking for her, "Are you in love with her, Jimmy?" Jimmy just nodded yes. Kevin continued, "I am in love too with this woman, but she never called me."

Jimmy replied, "Why don't you call her? You could ask her for a date."

Kevin answered, "I have never had to do that before. Women call me. I am God's gift to women. I am very cute and handsome. Who has sex with you and then never calls again?"

Jimmy looked at Kevin and then said, "Men do that all the time and think nothing of it. They have sex with a woman and never call them again. Kevin, you are not that cute. Call her."

Kevin replied, "I can't. I don't know her name. What is the reason you don't call the woman you love?"

Jimmy answered, "I don't want her to be afraid of me. I haven't told her how I feel about her."

Kevin said, "Boss, you are a rich, handsome guy and have everything to give her. What is there to be afraid of?" Jimmy didn't answer and just stopped talking. But when they got home, he had Mickey look up the week Kevin had taken off of work. Jimmy was sure that was the week. He would find out where Kevin was and then find the waitress that Kevin loved.

Kevin was to take the day off to take his kids to see their grandparents. Kevin was sure Alice's parents were trying to turn Calvin against him, so he went with this time. Sam was to watch Jimmy. They were driving around anywhere, and Sam had no idea what they were doing until Jimmy stopped the car to go into a place. Sam followed Jimmy into a Wilco food store. Was Jimmy hungry? Then Sam saw Jimmy just standing there, unable to move to look at a blonde hair woman who bounced all over when she walked. The woman smiled at Jimmy and then she took some black hair rollers to the checkout. Sam just called Kevin to get over there.

Kevin was there in a flash and said, "Boss, is everything okay?" Jimmy didn't hear Kevin and bought some black hair rollers. Kevin could smell the fine baked foods in the store and tried to get Jimmy to even look at the food, but Jimmy was out of the store looking for the woman.

Kevin said, "Do we need to get some cream on her face with the black hair rollers. Is that what turns you on with a woman? I get turned on with a woman who complains a lot."

Jimmy just looked at Kevin then said, "That is more information than I ever want to know about you. Please never talk to me again about it. But it does explain why you married Alice."

Sam had told the guys about the woman in the store and Jimmy. Then Cindy started to wonder was this her mother? If the woman smiled at her dad then why did they not date? Cindy wondered why parents make everything so complicated, and it was a surprise the kids were ever born. Cindy was worried if this was her mom, then how would she get her parents back together. If Cindy let it up to the guys, they would grab her by the hair dragging her home.

Cindy called the guys and the kids together to find a way to get this woman for her dad. Kevin said, "Cindy, your dad is in love with her. I got divorced and cheated on so I am not saying."

T-Jay said, "Sally's dad tried to kill Sam and I. We had to clean out many pig barns."

Mickey said, "I laid in front of the bus and almost stopped breathing for my woman."

Sam said, "I got to know Vicki and got her candy, flowers, with diamonds. That worked for me."

Cindy said, "Okay, that is what we do. We find out where she goes and get dad to go there too. Get them to talk, and he can get her candy, flowers, and diamonds. I think dad would do that." They had a plan; now they were going to look for her car to get her license number and find her.

Jimmy walked in and said, "What is the plan? I hope you are not talking about me. I need my space." No one said a word about it. Jimmy and Kevin continued driving around looking for her. Then one day, someone shot at the car and hit Jimmy on the side of his head.

The bullet didn't hit his head but just glanced it. Kevin whisked Jimmy out of there to Michael very fast. Sam and the guys got down there, but Margo with Aaron was no place in sight. Had Margo hired someone or was it just a crazy driver with a gun? The guys could not find out, but Jimmy was down for awhile. The last thing you want to do is hurt a genius' head. The president of the United States of America was on the phone with Kevin. He wanted to see Jimmy in Washington DC.

What did Jimmy do for the country? Jimmy was a scientist but what they did no one knew. Kevin said, "Jimmy has had issues with some presidents." The guys wanted to know more so Kevin got out his phone and said, "Tim helped me get the information from the tapes you guys watched. It started with that president whose wife was decorating the White House. See, there was no chair so Jimmy sat on the only chair and she sat on his lap facing him. Her husband walked in and said, me my mo." Mickey took Kevin's phone and played it again, and that president said, "You said what about Marylin and me, look at you."

Kevin continued, "His Vice President became President, and they were hunting at this ranch see, Jimmy is helping his wife shoot out the window." The guys looked, and the president was out that window that they were shooting out. Kevin continued, "Then, Jimmy and Tim were invited to the next president's daughter's wedding, but Jimmy got confused when the pastor said you may kiss the bride. Jimmy must have heard kiss the bride's mother, so he did, that president never looked happy anyway. Then there was the president whose wife had all those rehabs for drunks and Jimmy with her danced cheek to cheek. Don't get the wrong idea it wasn't the face cheek. That president just fell a lot. Next, Jimmy was praying with another president's wife, and they prayed different, so she had her arms around Jimmy. The next President liked his wife to wear red all the time. See, they are out watching the stars. Jimmy has his hands around her, so she doesn't fall, and the president is looking up."

Mickey looked again and said, "He is sleeping. Continue Kevin."

Kevin said, "Okay, the president, who was not going to raise taxes and used which P word will notice his wife is checking Jimmy here for an ear infection which is why Jimmy has his head on her lap. Then there is the president that called Jimmy a womanizer. Now he was a womanizer himself so he should know what one is. Jimmy was staying overnight in the Lincoln bedroom, and that first ladies was whispering stuff about other countries. It does looked like Jimmy is kissing her nick, but I am sure they were talking about other countries top secret stuff. Then there was the issue in the kitchen with that southern wife of that president, and it looked a little bad that Jimmy got his finger caught in the cookie jar. That is when Jimmy was told not to come to the White House anymore by that president. So Jimmy met the next president's wife in the Rose Garden, and she gave Jimmy a long-stemmed red rose which Jimmy smelled and kissed it. She also kissed the rose at the same time. I call this the rose kiss and that president was not pleased with Jimmy. He had to work with his Vice President those years. So I have to get Jimmy out of going to the White House. He is just sick."

No one said another word, but Jimmy came out and took Kevin's phone then smashed it on the floor with his foot. Kevin said, "I'm telling the Pope on you." Kevin started to write something, and Jimmy broke Kevin's pencil in half, then Jimmy just left the room.

Kevin said, "Jimmy's head must be hurting. He has just to lay down and go nowhere." The guys agreed.

A few weeks later, the kids were home from school and Sarah went into Jimmy's office saying, "I want T-Jay to take me to this university dance before I graduate. I have asked him, but he didn't answer me. T-Jay doesn't talk much. Make him do it. I want T-Jay to be my boyfriend."

Jimmy replied, "T-Jay is a friend, and we work together. I will not make him do anything, but I will talk to him about this." Jimmy always gave his kids what they wanted but could he give T-Jay to Sarah? Jimmy asked T-Jay to come into his office. Sam and Mickey listened at the door.

Jimmy said, "Kevin, you can go away now." So Kevin went out and listened too, but the guys climbed on the roof over Jimmy's office to hear better, so Kevin did too. Jimmy continued, "T-Jay, please sit down. I need someone to take Sarah to a dance at her school. Could you do that for me? The boys these days are out for only one thing, and this is my little girl. You understand?"

T-Jay's eyes were so wide open, and he said, "I know nothing about school dances. I never dated but with Sally only. I have not been close to anyone since Sally died. Maybe Kevin would be better. Kevin is closer to Sarah's age. Sarah has touched my face again and took my hand."

Jimmy smiled and said, "Kevin has the morals of an alley cat. Sally has been dead a few years now. Maybe this would help you, and I will talk to Sarah about the touching of you, okay." T-Jay nodded okay. T-Jay never said no to Jimmy on anything so he would take Sarah to this dance.

Sam and Mickey got off the roof right away, but Kevin's pants got caught on something, so he took his pants off and climbed down as Jimmy and T-Jay came out of the office. Mickey and Sam were off at a distance, laughing as Jimmy and T-Jay stopped to look at Kevin standing there without his pants. They looked up and saw Kevin's pants on the roof. Jimmy said to T-Jay, "Don't ask. Kevin is just different. He was possibly praying up on the roof and don't ask why." They just walked away saying no more, and Kevin got his pants down from the roof.

The dance was not so bad, and Jimmy had Mickey, Sam with their wives went as guests. Jimmy made sure the school would be okay with it with a large donation. All went well. Jimmy, Kevin, Michael with Marie, and the kids went to watch and then left early. Sarah had a wonderful time, and now she was telling Jimmy that she was in love with T-Jay.

At Sarah's graduation from college she was a little younger than most because she was very smart and ahead of her class, Jimmy said to T-Jay, "You and Sarah are getting along very nicely."

T-Jay replied, "Your daughter, Sarah, is so grown up and smart. She loves the color white. I would like your okay for me to date Sarah." T-Jay stepped back, and he was worried.

Jimmy said, "Where do you see this going between my daughter, Sarah and you?"

T-Jay replied as he took a few more steps back, "I would like to marry Sarah if that would be okay with you?" Then Kevin saw Sam and Mickey in a car for the getaway if Jimmy got mad.

Jimmy answered, "Okay, I am good with that but just don't wait too long to get married." After that things moved fast and on Sarah's next birthday, T-Jay got down on one knee with a diamond and asked Sarah to marry him. Sarah said yes and was crying, but she looked at Jimmy. He just winked at Sarah, and she smiled. Jimmy then had Kevin rewrite his Will that if he died that Sarah and T-Jay would care for Cindy along with Michael and Marie. Jimmy needed someone older on his Will, and T-Jay was perfect as Sarah's husband. Kevin did as Jimmy told him to. The wedding happened as soon as possible. The guys were sure Sarah must be pregnant, but T-Jay said that they never did that. Then why, until Kevin let them know about Jimmy's Will.

T-Jay made a mistake to see Margo and ask for her blessing on their wedding, his and Sarah's. Margo screamed at T-Jay saying, "You old fart will never marry my daughter Sarah. Over my dead body." Sam and Mickey were waiting in the car and then got T-Jay out of there before Margo could hit him. Sarah noticed something was upsetting T-Jay and Sam with Mickey were sure to tell her all about it. Jimmy had once said the guys gossiped more than church women.

Sarah went to Jimmy and Jimmy called T-Jay into his office. T-Jay came in like the world was all against him. Jimmy said, "So Sarah's mom, my ex-wife, doesn't approve of you marrying Sarah. Well, that makes this even better. You will make a great son-in-law for me, and I am paying for the wedding. I will be on cloud nine, walking Sarah down the aisle to marry you against Margo's wishes. Nothing could make me happier." T-Jay now was laughing too, and all he needed was Jimmy to approve of him marrying Sarah. Sarah wanted a big wedding which was great for Jimmy. The wedding would be in the winter, the first weekend of December at the place Jimmy and Marci had a home together with the white-haired people. Margo couldn't come there without help from Jimmy, so it was safe, she would not be able to make a scene. Jimmy did send an invite to Margo, Aaron, and their twins to come.

Kevin then called to see if they were coming and Margo said, "Over my dead body." Hung up.

Kevin said, "So that is a no on the four of you attending Sarah and T-Jay's wedding." Kevin could hear screaming in the background, so maybe the phone was not off, or she screamed that loud.

Halloween and Thanksgiving were all about the wedding. The girls were so happy and planned this big wedding. T-Jay was okay with all of it and just stayed with Jimmy. The wedding day came, with white flowers everywhere. Jimmy walked Sarah down the aisle and gave her away to T-Jay. They were both in white, and everything was white. The pastor married them and they stayed there for their honeymoon. Jimmy took all the guys home. Sam and Mickey were sure T-Jay needed their help, but Jimmy said. "No, he has done this before."

Michael now wanted to marry Marie. Michael went to Jimmy soon after Sarah and T-Jay's wedding. Marie had caught the flowers the bride threw to see who would marry next. Michael said, "I love Marie and always will, she is the only one for me. I want to marry as soon as possible. Please understand waiting is not easy for me." Jimmy agreed with Michael. Kevin just sat down, what was Jimmy thinking, he didn't need Michael to be married for his Will.

Jimmy replied, "I understand, son. But Marie is my adopted daughter and you better be good to her or I will hurt you, son. I know how much you love her and I want you to be with the woman you love, always." Then Michael and Jimmy with Cindy picked out a diamond ring for Marie. Michael carried that ring in his pocket all summer until his birthday which he always shared with Marie for she didn't know when she was born or to who. All Marie remembered was living on the streets and being so hungry until Jimmy's family found her, taking her to their home.

Michael had red roses all over the place in the garden where he took Marie and got down on one knee asking, "Will you marry me? I love you so much." Marie cried and agreed. Everyone was so happy for them. Cindy could help plan another wedding. Cindy thought she was big now because she had done all the church things but marry herself. Who would Cindy marry?

Calvin said, "Come on, we all know that Cindy is in love with C-Jay and C-Jay is in love with Cindy and Jimmy is completely okay with that. Betsy will marry Micky, and I need to find my true love, that little girl I met so long ago. Mickey, have you found out where my dad was, the name of the place?"

Mickey said, "I am so sorry, I forgot with all this going on. I will get right to it." Within days Mickey handed Jimmy the café and a name of the woman Kevin spent a week with along with his kids. Jimmy said nothing but studied it before showing it to Kevin and Calvin. The only thing different was this woman had two kids. Betsy started to add up the time, and it could be that she had another half-brother. Calvin just cared about the daughter. Kevin was going to talk to her and see if he could start the relationship all over again. Kevin was in love with her. Jimmy had Cindy and Betsy snuck in there when the family was asleep to find information which they did believe or not? Kevin went to see her with Jimmy and Calvin in the car. Betsy and Cindy hid in the house to hear what would happen.

Kevin knocked on the door with yellow roses and a box of candy. She opened the door and slammed it in Kevin's face. Kevin pushed in and said, "I am sorry I didn't call you, but I had my reasons. I would love to see you again. Here are some candy and flowers." She took the flowers and threw them at Kevin. He picked up the flowers and put them on the table. Then Kevin kissed her on the lips hard. She slapped him on the face. The girl and little boy were watching. Kevin asked, "Is that my son?"

She said, "Get out of here and never come back. I don't need you or want you." The kids hid.

Kevin replied, "I will leave because you have told me to go, but I will be back. I can leave some money to help."

Out the door Kevin went to the car, and Jimmy asked: "How did it go?"

Kevin replied, "Better than I thought it would go." And they went home. Betsy wanted to know if that little boy was her half-brother. Betsy was sure she was right, and the little boy was her new half-brother as Calvin was her half-brother.

Calvin said, "At night we will go as they are all sleeping and take a DNA sample from the boy. I want to see the daughter. I want to know if she is my true love." So the kids did, and it was Kevin's son. On Thanksgiving, Betsy decided she was going to tell Kevin, her dad. All the guys were there to hear this. But Marie was crying in the church and at their house. Cindy came in.

Cindy asked, "What is wrong? Do you not want to marry my brother, Michael?"

Marie cried harder and showed Cindy a letter from Margo which said that Margo didn't want Marie to marry her son, Michael because she was sure Marie could not have children from the lack of eating in her younger days. Margo was a doctor, so maybe she was right. Margo continued, Jimmy would want a grandson to carry on his name, Elgin. Cindy went to Jimmy.

Jimmy came into the church and said, "Marie, you are my adopted daughter, and I love you as I do all my children. You have helped us so much, and Michael needs you. I don't care if you have children or not. Sarah and T-Jay don't want children, and I am okay with that. I don't need you and Michael to have children. I have a granddaughter and son already. But let's not tell anyone that for now. My last name was a friend of mine's name Tim. So I don't care about having someone carry on a name that isn't mine."

Marie stopped crying and said, "Will you walk me down the aisle like you did Sarah and give me away to Michael?"

Jimmy replied, "I would love to do that, and I will be paying for the wedding so have what you want."

Cindy asked, "So I don't need to give you grandchildren either?"

Jimmy replied right away, "No, I will be needing seven grandchildren from you,

Cindy." Jimmy was not laughing. Was he telling Cindy the truth? Jimmy never really lied. Cindy was speechless.

Calvin went to tell C-Jay. Calvin said, "Jimmy will want seven grandchildren from Cindy. Are you up for that? Maybe Michael could give you vitamins to be sure. You know we never say no to Jimmy about anything." C-Jay just sat down and was thinking hard. How did Calvin know he loved Cindy? C-Jay had told no one and Cindy might not even love him. She was Jimmy's favorite daughter and child in the whole world; she looked like Jimmy's true love.

At the Thanksgiving, Betsy had told her dad, Kevin, about the little boy in the house was his son. The guys were laughing at Kevin's surprise. Calvin said, "Dad, don't mess this up. I love the daughter. She is my only true love forever." Jimmy sat down with the family to hear. Marie and Michael's wedding was small and in an out of way place. It was in Rome, and only the guys with their families were there. Margo, Aaron and the boys not even invited. It was a spring wedding, and for the honeymoon, they went to Mexico. Jimmy gave Marie away to his son, Michael. Then it was back to work as always, but Jimmy left to go to church without anyone. Jimmy just drove a car to a church, but on the way home the car started on fire as if someone had put a bomb on the passenger side. Kevin had been going crazy looking for Jimmy, and he found him just in time. Jimmy had escaped out of the car as it when into flames.

Kevin came running and said, "Boss, are you okay, why would you do that?"

Jimmy didn't want to talk about it, but Kevin wouldn't take no for an answer. So Jimmy said, "I followed her into that church. I am in love with her. And I know I shouldn't have done that."

Kevin promised, "I will tell none of the guys, but we have to move, and I want to make the new home secure. Somewhere they put the bomb under your car. But how would they know you were going to go into a church you have never been to before? Or have they hired a woman who looks like your true love to lead you into there and then planted the bomb?" Jimmy just agreed to have Kevin build a new house for them in Seattle. The house would look so much like the area unless you knew it was there, you would not see it. Would it look like a spaceship or was it? Jimmy had been on the government group called the Majestic Twelve. This group was to watch for aliens for the USA government. Jimmy was the leader of the group. Kevin thought, if a guy is an alien from another planet wouldn't someone tell him? They just had skills that Jimmy maybe invented for he was a genius. How Jimmy did this, he was not sure.

Jimmy kept going back to that church until he found her again going into the church but this time, Kevin was with him. Jimmy went and sat by the woman. She appeared not to know Jimmy at first, but then she said, "Do we know each other? Did we dance together all night awhile ago?"

Jimmy smiled and replied, "Yes. Do you remember me? I am Jimmy Elgin. We need to talk."

But church started, and everything was going okay until it came to the sign of peace, and Jimmy kissed the woman on the mouth. She was surprised and said, "Sir, we don't kiss people like that unless they are married to each other."

Jimmy replied, "Marry me then." The pastor was standing there watching them.

Kevin said, "Pastor, I think you should talk to these two after church. I can write down the questions you need to ask them."

Jimmy said, "Kevin, I thought you were here to help me look good. How are you doing that?"

Kevin replied, "I always do something stupider than you did but tonight that is not possible."

After church, Jimmy and the woman tried to sneak out of the church, but Kevin called out to the pastor, "They are over here. They are trying to sneak out of church without talking to you." From the look on Jimmy's face, he could have just killed Kevin, but over to the pastor, they went.

The pastor asked, "How long have you two known each other?"

The woman looked at Jimmy and said, "Don't lie to him."

Jimmy replied, "I would never lie to a pastor."

She whispered to Jimmy, "You are not going to tell him the truth?"

Jimmy said, "I wouldn't dream of doing that. Kevin help." So Kevin started talking to the pastor about the weather as Jimmy, with the woman got out of the church, and Jimmy walked her to her car. They got her license plate number off of her car. Now Jimmy could start dating her.

As Kevin got out to Jimmy by her car, Jimmy had just asked, "Could we go out on a date?"

She replied, "I am not in good health, I have everything wrong with me. Do you have any more questions?"

Jimmy replied, "Just one, can you still have sex?" Kevin just stood there saying nothing.

The woman answered, "Yes, but I have not had sex in a very long time. I think I forgot how."

Jimmy said, "I have not had sex for a very long time either, but I still know how. I go over it in my mind all the time." The woman just shook her head and drove away. Jimmy called, "Is that a yes, no, or maybe on the date?" Then Jimmy looked at Kevin and asked, "How did I do?"

Kevin replied, "Okay, boss and we got her car license plate so we can now find her for you." They went home, but Jimmy was going to take this slow with the woman he loved. Kevin was going to do a DNA test on her water she was drinking that he took from the church. Kevin took the DNA from Sylvia that Tim had left him and gave it to Michael. Cindy wanted Michael to test to see if this woman was her mother. Michael did and yes she was Cindy's physical mother, and she was Sylvia. Now Kevin understood Jimmy's love for her and why he did silly things to be with her. They had to help him, and Kevin was still working on his love for the waitress. This waitress complained more than any woman Kevin had ever known, and it was true love for him. Jimmy had an idea to have this waitress work for him part-time for some extra money, and she agreed. Kevin would have to train her, so then Kevin could see his son.

Calvin knew that the daughter was the little girl he had loved for so long, but he too was going slow with her.

Cindy had all kinds of questions for Jimmy about her mother. Cindy asked, "Why does she not always remember you? You are an unforgettable guy. Why did she not have me? Why did the two of you end it? Maybe she didn't want me? Was I the problem between you?"

Jimmy said, "Slow down, Cindy. Sylvia was hurt in a car accident when I was driving. So her parents took her away and told her I was just a dream. She was too sick to know it was real. I met her at a hospital when I was learning to be a doctor. You have an older full sister. I thought Sylvia died in childbirth with your brother Travis, but she didn't. Kevin found that out. I went to look for her and when I found her we, well, we had you, but Sylvia's health was so bad she could not carry you in her, so I was going to put you in Sally, C-Jay's mom. But Margo called, and I was afraid she would hurt Sarah, Michael, and Marie, so I went there first. I ran out of time to take care of you. Sylvia was okay with it, she wanted you and to see you at Sally's place." Jimmy looked tired so Kevin came in to take Cindy away, so Jimmy could rest.

Jimmy and Sylvia started talking on the phone each morning and before they fell asleep. Jimmy did give Sylvia flowers and candy, but she would not take diamonds from him nor money to pay bills he knew she had to pay. Sylvia started coming to the house, but only to Jimmy's office and then one night, Kevin got up to hear something. Jimmy was not alone in bed, there was someone with those black-haired rollers sleeping beside him, Sylvia? She had oxygen on at night to sleep, and it looked like Jimmy had set it all up for her, which did explain the new hospital-like bed Jimmy just had to have. Kevin was worried, what if Sylvia would die? The way Jimmy was holding his Sylvia, there would be no taking her away from him. Jimmy would hit you when you took food off his plate that he was eating. Taking Sylvia out of his bed, dying to try? He would kill you if you tried to take Sylvia away from him.

The guys were worried. Michael, said, "I think dad is too old for sex." Kevin didn't know what to do.

Cindy walked in and said, "Michael, why don't you tell dad he is too old for sex. I would love to see you do that." After that, no one said a word about Jimmy's overnight guest, but when Sylvia didn't come, Jimmy was noticeably hard to be around.

Kevin said, "We don't want Jimmy to leave us, and he will look for her. So be very nice to Sylvia." Cindy had her fifteen birthday with just C-Jay, and Jimmy was there at the place where Marci had once lived with Jimmy. It was fun and a big day for Cindy, but she was not sure why.

Jimmy had wanted Sylvia to come in the worse way, and she did for a little while on that December 21, 2012. The first time Cindy met her biological mother.

Sylvia had brown eyes like Cindy, dark blonde hair like Cindy. Sylvia smiled a lot and appeared to be very much in love with Jimmy as he was with her. Cindy had the best birthday gift of all, seeing her parents so in love.

That night, Jimmy and Cindy did something with a missile or bomb C-Jay noticed, but what was it? Jimmy had already taken Sylvia home. Jimmy came back and they shot something out into space. Was there a meteor or an object going to hit the planet Earth? Was the Maya December 21, 2012, really something true? Later on, the news reported in February, that broke apart objects had fallen in Russia. Did Jimmy and Cindy save Earth that day from its end and no one even knew it?

Things were going well for the first time in a long time. Jimmy had his Sylvia, Calvin had his true love, the daughter of the woman from that café, Jay. Kevin was trying to work something out with the woman named Mary from the café whose real name was Teresa Mary. Jimmy and Kevin went to eat where Teresa Mary worked, and Jimmy made her an offer that she couldn't say no to. Teresa Mary was to work for Jimmy as a business manager. She had the college degree but had never done any job but a waitress, so she never came to work for Jimmy. So, Jimmy told Teresa Mary, "This is good, I can train you the way I want you to do the work. Just a few half days a week. The pay is okay?" Teresa Mary agreed the pay was more than okay, it was great, and she needed the money for Teresa Mary would not take any money from Kevin. Teresa Mary came to report to work in Jimmy's office. The guys didn't like her right away. They said she smelled bad. She didn't dress right. She didn't know how to act right. Jimmy assigned Kevin to be Teresa Mary's trainer. So Kevin did what he knew, they had breakfast, coffee breaks, lunch, and long walks in the gardens. The guys complained more and questioned was she ever going to do any work around there? Time went by and there was no change.

Teresa Mary came at 10 AM, had breakfast with Kevin then went into Jimmy's office, but it was coffee break time, and then they went for a long walk in the garden and had lunch. Teresa Mary went home at 2 PM. This woman was overpaid and didn't do anything.

Sam said, "I want her job."

Mickey said, "No, I get her job."

T-Jay said, "I think you have to have sex with Kevin to get those hours." Both Sam and Mickey shook their heads, no thanks. Jimmy walked into the room and noticed the guys.

Jimmy called them into his office with Kevin and the kids; he said, "Who owns this business? I do, so I get to decide what my employees do? Who makes money here? I do, with your help, so I decide what I pay my employees and not you. So, if you don't like the way I run things around here, then you can leave and don't let the door hit you in the ass on your way out. Am I clear on this issue? Who needs to leave now? Kevin and Teresa Mary are doing a great job." No one left but they all knew Kevin was Jimmy's pet and his girlfriend was doing nothing.

Jimmy did spend time alone with Teresa Mary, and the guys' gossip was that something was going on there. Jimmy and Teresa Mary would talk for hours in his office without Kevin. They laughed about their mistakes in life and their bad choices in past lovers. But Kevin got to spend time with the son of Teresa Mary's which was his son too. The boy's name was Ricky, and he was a good kid. Kevin was trying hard to be a good father to little Ricky.

Ricky asked Kevin, "Are you my daddy? Are we rich? Can I have more toys?"

Kevin laughed and answered truthfully, "Yes, I am your daddy. Yes, I have more money than I need and you can have anything you want." Ricky hugged him. Kevin read stories to Ricky and took him to the movies. Jimmy had gotten Teresa Mary work clothes and helped with behavior around the office. Teresa Mary was not to smoke at work or drink liquor. That made her smell bad.

A few years went by, and it did look like Teresa Mary was doing something there. Jimmy's desk was organized, and Jimmy was in a better mood. No more moody time for Jimmy now that Sylvia was in his bed most nights. Calvin was trying to be a best friend to Jay and date her. Kevin tried to be a father to Ricky. Things looked good, Betsy was dating Micky and Cindy was dating C-Jay.

Then one day without warning Teresa Mary came into Jimmy's office and said, "Do you know of a doctor I can go and see about the birth control pill?" Jimmy and Teresa Mary did talk a lot.

Jimmy replied, "Don't want any more children? Don't want Kevin's children? What is up?"

Teresa Mary replied, "I have to clean up my act first before I can think about any more children. My drug and liquor issues are a problem. I love Kevin, and he is very good to me, but he forgets birth control most of the time."

Jimmy looked pleased and gave the name of a woman doctor he had the girls use. Teresa Mary set up an appointment and when she said Jimmy's name Teresa Mary got an appointment that day. So she went, but the woman doctor asked Teresa Mary, "Which daughter are you of Jimmy's?" Teresa Mary noticed the doctor was looking at her records and blood work. So she just smiled at the doctor and questioned was there something in her file or was it just a guess?

That night, Teresa Mary asked Calvin to help her break into the doctor's office so she could read what was in that file. Calvin didn't want to say no to her because she was Jay's mom, so he went along with it. Little Rickey stayed in the car. Teresa Mary couldn't get the door open, but Jay had told her mom that Calvin could get into the place without a key. Calvin let himself in the back door when they were not looking. Calvin opened the front door for them, and Teresa Mary went right for the doctor's files to find her file. The police came and saw little Ricky alone in the car, and they came inside to find Teresa Mary there.

Calvin grabbed Jay and poofed them away, but Tessia Mary was taken to the police station and booked for breaking into that doctor's office. Calvin told Kevin right away and Jay was very upset and confused. Michael gave her something to calm down and sleep. Marie stayed with Jay as Calvin sat outside her bedroom door. Kevin went down to the police station with Jimmy. Jimmy just sat back and let Kevin do his work.

Kevin took Ricky with him and showed the police his DNA report. So little Ricky got to stay with Kevin who had him sit by Jimmy. Kevin worked to get Teresa Mary out of that jail cell until she went to court for breaking into her doctor's office. Kevin paid a great deal of money, but he got Teresa Mary out of jail that night and home in her bed to sleep. She had to appear in court the next day. Teresa Mary was very happy with Kevin saving her, but then she read her file.

In the morning, Teresa Mary was in Jimmy's office as Jimmy walked in she screamed, "Why didn't you tell me that you are my father? Why didn't my mother tell me? Did Kevin know?"

Jimmy just sat down as Kevin walked to see what the hell was going on. Jimmy looked up at Teresa Mary and said, "I was going to, but it just wasn't the right time. Your mother forgets things, and she is very sick physically. Kevin didn't know."

Teresa Mary said, "When the hell were you going to tell me? Why didn't I get to have all that money your other kids have? Why did I have to live with nothing? My mother is not that sick." Jimmy just sat there, and Kevin could see Jimmy was losing his temper with Teresa Mary.

Jimmy replied, "Teresa, you have been a real bitch to your mother, and that stops right now. How much money do you think is yours? You can have it right now. But as for you having nothing, it's just wrong. The man that raised you loved you as a daughter, and I think he did a better job than I ever could have done. He gave you more than I ever could have which was all his love and everything he had. You should always love and respect him as I do. So how much money do you want from me? I guess money is all that ever mattered to you? Kevin, she is all yours." Then Jimmy just walked out of his office. Kevin held Teresa Mary close.

Kevin whisper, "I have enough money for us. But you have to tell Jimmy you are sorry."

Teresa screamed, "Never, I hate him and you too. You will never see my children or me again."

Kevin looked at Teresa Mary with loving eyes but said, "Then I will not get you off of the charge of breaking into that doctor's office so you will go to jail. I will take our son, Ricky and Jay can live with her grandparents, Jimmy and Sylvia. Is that what you want?"

Teresa Mary cried, "No."

Kevin said, "I will get you off with no jail time or cost, but you will be nice to your mother and tell Jimmy you are sorry for the way you talked to him. Jimmy is not just my boss. He is my best friend. I will not choose between you two. You are wrong here, my love. I may not be the best father in the world to my kids, but I know being a father is not just about money for kids."

Teresa Mary was still upset, but she didn't want to go to jail, and Kevin did get her off with a few years of probation. Jimmy did offer Teresa Mary money, but she didn't take it, so Jimmy put some money in accounts for his granddaughter Jay and grandson Ricky with Kevin's help as a lawyer. The first year was stressed, but then things started to settle down. Teresa Mary was Jimmy's business manager with Kevin as his lawyer, and all the guys with kids knew Teresa Mary was Jimmy's oldest daughter. Sarah and Michael had some issue with it but not Cindy.

Things got back to going well until that Thanksgiving when Micky asked Kevin at the dinner table, "Mr. Carlson, I would like your daughter's hand in marriage?" Kevin looked around for his father who was Mr. Carlson then he saw the boy was talking to him and want to marry his baby daughter, Betsy. He got up from the table and went into the kitchen where he turned on the oven to put his head in it. Jimmy came in after to pull Kevin out of the oven.

Jimmy said, "Kevin, we have electric ovens. Michael, please give Kevin a shot to calm him down." So Michael did. Jimmy then said to Micky, "Give Kevin a few days to answer you. I am sure he will be okay with it, give him some time." Micky agreed with Mickey and Virginia giving him support. It turned out Virginia wanted strawberry blonde grandchildren, and Mickey wanted whatever Virginia, his wife, wanted. Micky wanted to marry Betsy, and she wanted Micky. Kevin stayed in bed for three days, and Teresa Mary came to help Kevin who just cried with her.

Betsy asked Jimmy, "What was that shot Michael gave dad that hurt so bad he has been in bed for three days?"

Jimmy replied, "It was not the shot that hurt your dad, Kevin so much, it was just nature." Betsy was sure she understood, but maybe it was her getting married and not being a little girl anymore. Jimmy went to talk with Kevin, and said, "Kevin your daughter,

Betsy could do worse and marry an alien from another planet. I think Micky we know and his dad Mickey works here."

Kevin's mind was going in all direction, and he thought, If I am an alien and so are my children, wouldn't Jimmy tell me? But Kevin knew Jimmy never lied, however, he didn't like to talk about something which he didn't do, even if he should have. Like telling Teresa Mary that she was his daughter or telling Kevin. Maybe Kevin was too stressed over this, and it was nothing. So Kevin agreed to let Betsy marry Micky, but they had to sign a paper saying they would always live with Kevin. They never denied any visitation rights to his forthcoming grandchildren. Micky agreed right away, but Betsy took a little longer. Mickey was so happy with this idea, no grandchildren for him to have to care for and his wife could visit, just don't bring them home.

The wedding plans were on, and Cindy seemed sad. C-Jay was sure she wanted to get married too, but he was not sure if she wanted to marry him. Then he would have to ask Jimmy. Cindy was Jimmy's little angel and Jimmy may kill him for even asking to marry his baby girl. C-Jay went to Calvin for help. Calvin said, "Don't you have any friends to talk to? I know nothing about women or girls. I am still trying to date Jay and marry her one day. She is my true love."

C-Jay said, "I have to talk to Jimmy, please help me." Calvin made a sound and then took C-Jay to listen at Jimmy's office door. Kevin and Jimmy were talking about Betsy's wedding.

Jimmy said, "Are you sure you want Betsy and Micky to live with you forever? You may regret that one day."

Kevin replied, "Never. Do you want Cindy to marry and move away?"

Jimmy answered, "Yes I do. I want all my children to move away and let me live my life without them telling me I am too old for sex or anything. I want to be alone with Sylvia. Maybe she would go into other rooms besides my bedroom and office if all these people would move out. And when is that C-Jay going to ask me if he can marry Cindy? I am not getting any younger."

Kevin replied, "I think C-Jay is afraid of you. Be nice." Jimmy agreed to be very nice. Then Calvin and C-Jay left the area with C-Jay thinking he better not waste any more time or Jimmy could find someone else to marry Cindy. C-Jay would go to Jimmy in the morning right away.

C-Jay entered Jimmy's office saying "Sir, do you have a minute?" Jimmy looked up and smiled.

Kevin said, "Jimmy is very nice and understanding." Then Kevin left the room, leaving C-Jay afraid.

C-Jay spoke, "I love Cindy and would like to ask her to marry me. Could I have your blessing?"

Jimmy replied, "Yes, but you should also get your father, T-Jay's blessing and Sylvia's blessing."

C-Jay answered, "Yes, sir, I will do that before I ask Cindy to marry me. She may say no." Jimmy just smiled and nodded okay. Out the door, C-Jay went as fast as he could so Jimmy could not change his mind. To Calvin, C-Jay went for more help.

Calvin replied "T-Jay is your dad. He will understand. Just talk to him about it. Don't you talk?"

The truth was that they didn't talk at all and C-Jay went to talk this over with his grandparents. They were happy and loved Cindy. That was Sally's parents, but C-Jay didn't know his dad's parents at all. They always sent cards and money or gifts, but he never saw them. C-Jay had Christmas cards from them with a picture of them, but that was it. Jimmy had said he only needed his dad and Sylvia's blessing. So C-Jay went to his dad's apartment on the top floor of Jimmy's house. He knocked on the door, the white door, they were the white people, and everything in their house was white. The floors, the walls, and the furniture were all white. Jimmy always wore dark glasses in their home. Too much white.

Sarah came to the door and let C-Jay in. They never really talked either, she was just the younger woman who married his dad. But Sarah was also Cindy's half-sister. T-Jay came out in white and said, "This is a first. Why are you here? Are you sick? Are your grandparents okay?"

C-Jay answered straight, "I want your blessing to ask Cindy to marry me." T-Jay stepped back.

Then he said, "Over my dead body. I brought you into this world, and I am going to take you out. That is boss' silver daughter, and you are not good enough to marry her." Calvin had heard all this and ran to C-Jay.

Calvin said, "Run and jump out the window or your dad will kill you."

C-Jay looked out the window and remembered they were on the top floor, so that was how many floors to jump out of and live? So he ran back to Cindy and told her all about it, after which she kissed him. Then together she poofed them out of there to her car, and they just drove away with T-Jay now running after the car. Sarah got T-Jay into their car, but by that time Cindy had lost them. C-Jay wondered why didn't Sarah chase after them. Now C-Jay thought more of Sarah that she was not just the younger woman who married his dad but a friend and family.

They drove to T-Jay's parents to ask for help. Cindy told them the truth that she loved C-Jay, and he loved her, but his dad didn't approve of them marrying. The grandparents came up with an answer, if they disapprove of the wedding then as always T-Jay would do the opposite. And have Sally's parents approve which they did, and T-Jay would do as they wanted. So the kids ate there and they prayed together about it, then set on their way to the other grandparents.

Sally's parents were in complete agreement, so they called T-Jay with their approval of the wedding. T-Jay's parents called him with their disapproval of the wedding. T-Jay agreed to give C-Jay his blessing to marry Cindy. Now all he needed was Sylvia's blessing but how would C-Jay find her? Cindy said, "Well, we know where Sylvia is almost every night, in my dad's bed. Go to his bedroom and ask her." There was no way C-Jay was storming into Jimmy's bedroom to ask Sylvia. There had to be another way. So C-Jay went to ask Calvin for help.

Calvin made a sound of displeasure, but he said, "I know Sylvia goes into the garden in the daytime. Watch for her in the garden when Jimmy is working in his office with my dad, Kevin."

So C-Jay waited days and at last Sylvia went into the garden. C-Jay walked up to her and said, "Sorry Miss Sylvia, but I need to ask you if I could have your blessing to marry your daughter, Cindy."

Sylvia smiled and answered, "Yes, thank you so much for even asking me. I love my daughter so much, and I know you love her too." Then Jimmy came out with a big smile and took Sylvia to his bedroom to rest. Jimmy was so in love with Sylvia anyone could see that.

Now C-Jay had all he needed but to ask Cindy, so we all know where he went for help, to Calvin. Calvin said, "Can't you do anything by yourself? Will I have to be there on your wedding night? Take a weekend like this one, Memorial weekend, and go to a place you both like. Maybe the farm of your grandparents. Cindy loves it there or the place where that Marci lived. Or maybe putting flowers on your mom's grave for the Memorial weekend, then down on one knee and ask her."

C-Jay said, "What if Cindy says no?"

Calvin replied, "I'll bet you one billion dollars Cindy will say yes. If not, you have a billion dollars to go away with and cry." C-Jay agreed.

C-Jay said, "What about the ring? I don't have much money. How do I know what she likes?"

Calvin replied, "Ask Jimmy about the ring. You have to tell him about the blessing anyway. Jimmy is at the place where he and Marci once lived. I'll take you there, now." So they left.

Jimmy was working in the office of Marci's when they got there. Calvin waited outside. He always felt at home here, and he was sure there were animals somewhere but had not seen any animals. Calvin went looking around. C-Jay went to talk to Jimmy. C-Jay said, "Calvin brought me up here to talk to you. I got all the blessings from my dad and Sylvia. But I don't know what kind of ring Cindy would want. Maybe she will say no to me."

Jimmy smiled and said, "I don't think Cindy will say no to you. I have a ring that has been in my family forever. My mother would like you to give it to Cindy for your wedding." Jimmy got a ring from an older white-haired woman who smiled at C-Jay. She looked very sick and weak, so they left right away, but she blessed C-Jay with the ring before Jimmy and C-Jay found Calvin.

Calvin was in a cave and said, "I saw winged horses with a horn on their noses. But the horse just poofed away."

Jimmy replied, "I just knew they were here. You and the kids find them and make peace with this winged, horned horse. I believe there are black, white, and red colored horses here."

That weekend, C-Jay took Cindy to the farm and then to his mom's grave where he got down on one knee and asked, "Will you marry me? I love you so much. Maybe this is not the right place to ask you that. This ring your father gave me from I think your grandmother, his mom."

Cindy answered, "Yes, I will marry you. And yes this is the ring from my grandmother, my dad, Jimmy's biological. It is the perfect place to ask me that with your mom here. Your mom and my mom were the best of friends. I love you, too." Then Cindy kissed C-Jay.

The other kids were up looking for the winged, horned horses. Calvin had Jay with them and little Ricky. A black winged horse let Jay on his back and flew away. Calvin followed after them and saw how beautiful the winged horse was, and Jay was with them as the horse drank water. Betsy loved the red horses but Cindy loved the white horses and kids visited the animals all the time. The kids only told Jimmy about the winged, horned horses and how they loved them.

Jimmy's mother died one day before Betsy's wedding with Jimmy and Cindy holding her hands. Jimmy was on her left and Cindy held her right hand. Sylvia was there to hold Jimmy's right hand. C-Jay on Cindy's left side was holding her left hand. Calvin was sure that meant something but what? Cindy would now do Marci's job; Jimmy had never replaced Marci but what about Marci's kids? Calvin wanted to figure it all out, but he too would never ask Jimmy about it.

A new president was elected. Jimmy with Kevin had to go to Washington DC, and this time Jimmy asked, "Calvin come with us but remember, this is a very evil place. This president is a quick learner." Kevin had Calvin wear a suit which was something he never really did, except for weddings.

Kevin said, "You will wear this suit. We Americans respect our president even if we may not agree with them or even voted for them." Calvin wore the suit and so did Jimmy with Kevin. The meeting was fast. Kevin had to go to the bathroom before it ended, but Jimmy was the one the president wanted to talk to Jimmy had mostly worked with the vice presidents because the other presidents would get mad at him for being too close to their wives. But this time, Jimmy had his Sylvia, so this president's pretty blonde wife was of little interest to Jimmy and that president knew it. After they were done, Jimmy and Calvin couldn't find Kevin.

Then after hours of looking, Kevin was found hiding behind the speaker's desk. Kevin was afraid to come out. Kevin said, "A creator tried to eat or have sex with me." Jimmy got Kevin into the plane and they went home, giving Kevin a shot to calm down.

Cindy asked, "Are we being invaded by aliens from outer space? Should we fight?"

Jimmy replied, "No, Kevin is afraid for all congresspeople. He thinks they are all evil, and he may be right, but they are just Democrats and Republicans. I told Kevin many times never read their minds, it will scare the hell out of you. No aliens are invading our capital, just evil."

Betsy had her wedding on a beautiful winter day in January the same day Micky's parents were married. Her colors were red and white, strawberries. Kevin did walk her down the aisle to Micky, in a church. Teresa Mary was there for Kevin, and he sat with her. Calvin, Jay, and Ricky were in the wedding party. They honeymooned where Jimmy's mom had lived and Marci. A place no one was sure where it was, but they could find it.

Cindy's wedding was next on June 21, but Jimmy had reminded C-Jay by saying, "I will be needing seven grandchildren from you and Cindy. I don't care what position you use to make the kids." Now C-Jay was all upset; he went to Calvin for more help.

C-Jay said, "You have got to help me with the seven grandchildren Jimmy wants from Cindy and I. He said he doesn't care what position we use to make the kids. I only know one way for sex."

Calvin replied, "This is the last time I am helping you. I will get you a book; it is in your mailbox." Calvin was true to his word and C-Jay could hardly look at it, but it showed everything. C-Jay had a church and house built for Cindy at his grandparents' farm, and they were married there. Jimmy walked Cindy down the aisle to C-Jay. Sylvia sat in front, waiting for Jimmy to sit by her. Cindy's colors were of the rainbow, and they stayed there on the farm for their honeymoon.

Now that all the kids were married but Calvin, who was waiting for his Jay to be older. If love was worth having, it was worth waiting for, and true love would never die. Calvin had learned from Jimmy's mistakes with Sylvia, and he could wait until it was right for both of them. Betsy came in and took the donut right out of Kevin's hands. Kevin smelled his hands where the donut once was. Jimmy said, "You just had to have those kids live with us forever. My little Debbie, powered donuts are for Sylvia and Calvin who get bad migraine headaches, it helps."

Michael said, "Dad, stop it, little Debbies are not health food. And these people look up to you."

Kevin replied, "Your kids are not leaving either. The home on the farm is Cindy and

C-Jay's vacation home. They are living here with everyone else." Jimmy cried, and Sylvia kissed him.

Calvin just smiled, he loved his family and friends, even if it was hard to believe or not. Maybe they were not aliens from another planet; maybe Calvin thought too much about Tim's unbelievable tall tales. They were a little different but believable family and friends. Calvin wondered if you become smart because you are born that way or is it because you are with smart people? Do you become what you see and do? They had been raised around Jimmy, a genius, and Cindy, but were all Jimmy's kids genius? Was Teresa Mary not smart or could she have been? So maybe it is who you are around and who your family brings into your world that makes you who you are. Calvin had always seen his dad, Kevin and Jimmy pray or read the bible, so he did. The Bible had the answers to everything, and there was a higher power, but it was not Jimmy. He was a guy like all men, and he made mistakes, but he tried and believed in God. Calvin would do the same and all Calvin wanted was to marry his true love, Jay. Because to Calvin, love is all that really matters in the long term and what you truly believe. Believe in yourself, your family, which we know is not perfect but we love them anyway. And we pray to a higher power of God for guidance and help. Because when a guy loves a woman or girl, he has to pray more. His true love is more than life itself. A guy leaves his parents to take a wife in love.

Calvin said, "I know, readers, the question you asked about the story, so I will answer it now for you. I got Marci's whip. I will not use it on my true love but in church, if you forget to put money in the collection box, watch out. Remember, I can read your mind. I know what you did."

THE END

Printed in the United States
By Bookmasters